The Merry Adventures of Harshabardhan and Gobardhan

by

Shibram Chakraborty

Translated by Arunava Sinha

hachette
INDIA

Shibram Chakraborty (1902–1980) wrote extensively for both children and adults, using his trademark humour and wordplay to tell stories about the peculiarities of human beings. His most memorable characters were the brothers Harshabardhan and Gobardhan – innocents from Assam who were endowed with plenty of money, thanks to their wood and furniture business, but not with the toughness needed to survive in the big bad city of Calcutta. Chakraborty was a free spirit who ran away from home as a boy, took part in the freedom movement and went to jail as a teenager – he never finished school – and lived alone in a boarding house in Calcutta most of his adult life. His stories are about eccentric people in absurd situations, and brim over with fun and puns. He wrote in Bengali.

Arunava Sinha translates classic, modern and contemporary Bengali fiction, non-fiction and poetry into English. Over two dozen of his translations have been published so far. His recent translations for children also include Satyajit Ray's *The Magic Moonlight Flower and Other Enchanting Stories* and Moti Nandy's *Kalabati, The Showstopper*. He was born in Calcutta and lives in Delhi.

The Merry Adventures of Harshabardhan and Gobardhan

First published in 2014 by Hachette India
(Registered name: Hachette Book Publishing India Pvt. Ltd)
An Hachette UK company
www.hachetteindia.com

SRD

ISBN 978-93-5009-748-9

Hachette Book Publishing India Pvt Ltd,
4th & 5th Floors, Corporate Centre;
Plot No. 94, Sector 44; Gurgaon 122003, India

Typeset in Bembo Std 11/14.4
By Eleven Arts, New Delhi

Printed and bound in India
by Manipal Technologies Limited, Manipal

FSC
www.fsc.org
MIX
Paper | Supporting responsible forestry
FSC™ C043100

A Note on the Translation

'In my stories I never considered children as children, as little babies who understand nothing. I considered them my equal. I treated them as adult friends. What they got from my stories were not moral lessons about growing up, but the taste of being grown-ups. Children love my stories because I don't write for children.'

No one could have explained Shibram Chakraborty's literature better. After all, this is the writer himself, talking about his work to an imaginary journalist. 'My writing is adulterated,' he punned, 'which is why it turns children into adults.' The fact is that the 20 stories in this book, like all of Chakraborty's work, neither include children in a big way, nor talk about things like good behaviour, the importance of school or obedience, which bore young people. Instead, they are about the somewhat silly behaviour of grown-ups. (Which, as we know, pretty much describes all adults.)

The bumbling brothers Harshabardhan and Gobardhan – Harshabardhan's wife also puts in an appearance – are the most enduring and endearing of Chakraborty's creations. They constantly make mistakes. They are taken for a ride by others. They turn petulant and begin to sulk, or simply lose their temper, when things don't go their way. And Chakraborty brings his inimitable brand of humour to all these situations and the way they were resolved.

Humour, in fact, was the cornerstone of the writer's life. Once, a fan of his stories who had encountered him on the street actually followed him to the boarding house he lived in – he never married or lived in a home of his own as an adult. There, Chakrabroty handed his guest some headache pills, advising him to take them quickly. 'But I don't have a headache,' the guest protested. 'You will soon, now that you've come to see me,' the writer assured him.

This could easily be a part of one of the numerous stories that Chakraborty wrote. He made his living as a writer, but it wasn't much of a living, since he gave stories to any publisher who asked for them, seldom bothering with payment. No one knows exactly how many stories he wrote (and he wrote for grown-ups too). The walls of his room were his account book – that was where he scrawled details of the money he had received, borrowed or lent. Naturally, few of the people he lent money to ever returned it to him.

Actually, Chakraborty lived the kind of independent, uncomplicated life that most of us can only dream of. He didn't own a house, a car or any of the trappings of modern existence. He walked to most places, ate at convenient restaurants, and didn't even own very many clothes. But he read and wrote prodigiously, although he pretended to be a very lazy man. In fact, when asked how his day went, he summed it up this way: wake up, have breakfast, which is tiring, so go right back to sleep, have lunch, rest, have afternoon tea, and so on until dinner and sleep. When do you write, then, he was asked by his incredulous listener. The next day, of course, he answered.

As here, it is always difficult to tell when Shibram Chakraborty is joking and when he's serious. Indeed, his stories, he claims, are not funny at all – it is only the telling of them that is funny. He may be right. Take the story with which he highlights how little money he had. A fellow writer once wrote a glowing tribute to him in a book of essays. When Chakraborty went to the publisher to pick up a copy of the book, the publisher apparently told him, what's the point, you'll only sell it at a second-hand bookshop, why don't you just take the price of the book instead in cash. Chakraborty apparently did just that.

And how did the publisher know this? Because, says the writer, he always sold the 25 free copies of his own book – which he was entitled to getting – back to the publisher to make some money. I hate reading as much as I hate writing, Chakraborty adds, explaining why his room was bereft of books.

Chakraborty's passion was the pun. Playing with words effortlessly, often using both Bengali and English, he created an entire way of telling stories through puns. Just one example: Harshabardhan's name often becomes an opportunity to talk about horses. Discovering the puns hidden in the dialogue – all his characters are adept punsters – and then translating them into English equivalents was great fun, even if it means preserving the 'punnyness' at the expense of the precise meaning.

In fact, translating these stories brought me to the brink of – and often crossing over – my self-imposed constraints of translating: remove nothing and add nothing. When transferring the groan-inducing puns from Bengali to English, it sometimes became necessary to shift the context and even the content of what Harshabardhan or Gobardhan might be saying, so that the pun might be preserved. I cannot help feeling that Chakraborty would not have minded, for he said, 'Words have always appeared mysterious to me. Each word is a world in itself.' The sound, he said, was as important as the meaning. And hence the importance of the pun over mere meaning.

Contents

1

Harshabardhan Goes to Mumbai

'I just got the telegram,' Harshabardhan told his brother. 'They've accepted all our conditions for supplying the timber. Get dressed, we're leaving at once.'

'Where are we going, Dada?' asked Gobardhan.

'Bombay.'

'What for?' Gobardhan or Gobra as he was fondly called looked like the sky had fallen on his head.

'Didn't you hear? The company in Bombay has accepted all our conditions. Let's go and finalize the contract. It's a juicy deal. They've asked me to go at once.'

Harshabardhan was a man of impulses. Gobardhan knew this, but still he stammered, 'How can we go at once, Dada?'

'If not now then when? We don't have much time before the train leaves. The *Bombay Mail* won't wait for us, will it? We have to leave at once.'

'What about a bath? Dinner?'

'We can bathe on the train. There are fantastic bathrooms. They have showers. As for dinner, there is marvellous food in the dining car.'

'Don't we have to take our bedding?'

'That's all part of the arrangements in the first-class compartments. Who on earth takes his own bedding into a first-class compartment? And in Bombay we'll stay at a plush hotel. They don't lack for beds there.'

'You don't want to take any luggage at all?'

'Luggage? Just the one piece. You. You are an entire piece of luggage all by yourself.'

Gobardhan was deeply hurt. So was his self-respect. But he couldn't summon a retort. He only grunted.

Harshabardhan changed his mind on the way to the station. 'No, on second thoughts, let's not go first class. The third class is good enough for us.'

'Why, aren't we rich enough?' Gobardhan protested vehemently. 'The rich always travel by first class.'

They aren't millionaires, they're sillyonaires. Older but no wiser. Haven't you read in the papers about the kind of trouble people face in first-class compartments? All the criminals jump into the train and rob and loot everyone. There are murders too. Is it a good idea to die helplessly? No, I'm not losing my brother just to travel first class.'

'Lose your brother! Why?'

'You'll try to save me if someone tries to kill me. I know you will. And you'll end up dying, that's not what I want.'

Gobardhan was silent.

'Besides, I might be able to bear my brother's loss, but my own loss would be a disaster. I'll never profit from it.'

Harshabardhan breathed a sigh of relief when they reached Howrah Station. 'I'll go buy the tickets.'

'The third class will be very crowded, Dada.'

'What crowd are you talking about? I'm going to reserve the entire compartment.'

Having done just that, Harshabardhan asked the ticket clerk, 'How long does the train stop at Agra?'

'At least half an hour. *Bombay Mail* meets *Calcutta Mail* there, you see . . .'

'*Calcutta Mail*! What on earth is the *Calcutta Mail*?' The brothers were astonished.

The train that leaves Bombay for Calcutta. That's the *Calcutta Mail*. Just like we have *Bombay Mail*,' explained the ticket clerk. 'Why did you want to know about Agra?'

'We were thinking of visiting the Taj Mahal. Is it possible?'

'Well, if you take a taxi from the station and finish it all off in half an hour, you can.'

'There are always taxis at stations,' said Gobardhan. 'So why not?'

Harshabardhan got into their compartment only to jump out again. 'Wait here, I'll be back in a minute.'

When he returned in a short while Gobra asked, 'What have you got, Dada? New snacks or a newspaper?'

Instead of answering, Harshabardhan held up a book to Gobardhan. It was neither food nor a newspaper. Gobra discovered to his utter surprise that the book was titled *The Wonders of Science*.

'I got it from a platform bookstall.'

'What's this for, Dada? This isn't a storybook.'

'A book about science,' Harshabardhan informed his brother. 'This is the age of science, did you know that?'

Eventually the train left. Without wasting any more words, Harshabardhan immersed himself in his book.

He floated up to surface a long time afterwards. 'Do you know why an apple falls from a tree to the ground?'

'Because it's ripened.'

'Says who? It could have flown away instead of falling to earth, couldn't it?'

'Do apples have wings?'

'My foot. It's all because of the force of gravity. Do you know what gravity is? Newton discovered it.'

'Newton? How?'

'I have no idea what Newton was like. Never saw him in my life. He died long before we were born. But gravity is something like this – Newton was skulking beneath an apple tree once . . .'

'With his mouth open?'

'Who can tell? The apple fell at that moment . . .'

'Into his mouth?'

'I don't know that either. But as a result gravity was discovered. Got it?'

'Got it. But it's not the force of gravity, it's the force of gravy.'

'It says gravity here . . .'

'Printing mistake. Books are full of such mistakes. Does gravi mean anything? Gravy does. And where does the gravy go? To the stomach. The stomach in my case, the paunch in yours – but they definitely have a force, which is hunger. Only you know what you do when you feel hunger in your paunch, but in my stomach . . . when the force of hunger asserts itself I can feel it. I go straight to our orchard. Our mango orchard, where I stare at the trees with my mouth open. And when the ripened mangos slip from the branches, I slip them into my mouth. I have felt this force of gravy – discovered it long ago. But I didn't go writing a book like your Newton to tell everyone.'

Harshabardhan was astounded by his brother's scientific temperament. Without responding, he immersed himself again in his book.

He made his second statement some time later. 'Do you know why the lid of the kettle rattles when you put it on the stove?'

'Only Newton knows.'

'Not Newton, someone else. Newton didn't do this one. The lid rattles so that it can run our trains one day.'

'Really?' Gobardhan's eyes were round saucers.

'Haven't you seen the vapour rising from boiling water? It's called steam. The pressure from the steam makes the lid rattle. It's the same steam that's packed into a train engine to make this huge train move. Got it?'

Gobardhan was speechless in astonishment.

'You're a lot like a kettle too. You're so restless I think you have a lot of steam inside you. Maybe you will run something big. You might run the country too. Or at least a train engine.'

'You're laughing at me, Dada. I may never work up enough steam, but you have to accept that people hold my intelligence in greater esteem than yours.'

'More than me? Really? Here, keep my wallet. It has a hundred hundred-rupee notes – ten thousand in all. Only if you can return it to me intact when we get out of the train at Bombay will I admit that you're not only intelligent but also in luck, because I will give you half the money as a prize.

'Are you saying I won't be able to keep it safe?'

'I'm betting half the money in there. I just hope the wallet stays in your pocket long enough. Cheats and thieves are swarming everywhere – they are all pickpockets. I'm positive your pocket will be picked when we get off at Agra and look for a taxi. Take my word for it.'

'Then I'm not putting it in my pocket at all. I'll tuck it into my belly. I'll use the force of gravy to hold on to it.'

Several stations flashed past. Beleaguered by the numerous wonders of science, Harshabardhan nodded off while Gobardhan went to the toilet.

He shot out screaming soon afterwards. 'Dada, Dada! Very bad news!'

'What is it!' Harshabardhan opened his eyes.

'I'd tucked the bag into my belly, remember? The moment I squatted on the toilet seat it escaped my force of gravy and slipped into the hole.'

'What? Why didn't you pull the chain at once? The train would have stopped instantly. We could have retrieved the bag by now.'

'I did! Everytime I pulled the chain, water flowed into the commode.'

'There goes the money – how unaccommodating.' But Harshabardhan did not sound even remotely peeved. 'Didn't I tell you you'd lose it? Saw how I won the bet?'

'Your money's lost,' grieved Gobardhan. 'Ten thousand. Ten!'

'Do you think I put all my money in one pocket?' Harshabardhan comforted his brother. 'I had four wallets in four pockets. I only gave you the one in my breast-pocket. See here, one in the right pocket, one in the left, and one in the inside pocket of my coat. How many can the pickpocket pick?'

Still Gobardhan was inconsolable.

'Don't be upset. Money's not for hoarding. We earn so that we can spend. Do I save my money? I throw it away. I love money too much – I can go to hell, but I won't let my money go there.'

When the train stopped at Agra, the brothers visited the Taj Mahal, ate *pooris* and sweets at the market, bought two pairs of locally famous shoes, and finally returned to the station as the train was about to leave, the guard having blown his whistle.

Running up to the train, they jumped into the first compartment they could.

It was practically empty apart from someone half-lying on an upper bunk. 'Are you going to Bombay too?' Harshabardhan began a conversation. 'Will you get off at Bombay?'

'No, I'm going to Calcutta,' he replied.

'Calcutta! How amazing!' Harshabardhan was thrilled. 'Look at this, Gobra. Another wonder of science, see for yourself. The lower bunks of this train are going to Bombay and the upper bunks to Calcutta.'

'These bunks have mattresses, Dada. Let's catch a little sleep.' Gobra was tempted.

'Good idea, let's do that. We've seen the Taj Mahal, we've eaten, we've even bought shoes. Might as well dream about the Taj Mahal now.'

When they rose from their long, deep slumber, they discovered that the compartment was empty and the train was standing at the terminus.

'Get off the train, Gobra. What are you staring at? We've reached.' Harshabardhan dragged Gobardhan out of the train, railing at him.

Down on the platform, the brothers were flabbergasted. They had expected to see a crowd of Marathis and Gujaratis and Punjabis, but everyone around them was a Bengali.

'They say Bengalis are a stay-at-home lot. They say people from all over flock to Bengal to make a living, but Bengalis don't like going anywhere. But it's just the opposite here . . .'

Outside the station they discovered more reversals.

'Oh look! They've built a bridge just like the Howrah Bridge here too!'

'Just look at the marvels of science, Dada!' Gobra was no less astounded. 'They've got the Ganga from Calcutta to Bombay.'

'I'd expected to see a new city. But this is a replica of Calcutta. Why bother to go on such a long journey to Bombay if the *Bombay Mail* only brings us to another Calcutta?'

'Tchah!' Even Gobardhan, overcome with grief, expressed his dismay. 'Our Calcutta is much better, Dada.'

'Of course it is,' Harshabardhan agreed. 'Haven't you heard of Mumbai ka *bhel*? This Bombay Mail has shown us some *bhelki* alright. Magic. It's brought us back to the same Calcutta that we came from.'

2

Harshabardhan's Farsightedness

The Assam government had sent a notice to every Assamese including Harshabardhan. Although he had left Assam for Calcutta long ago to start a timber business, he had not been able to escape the strict eye of the government of Assam.

Not just him, his brother Gobardhan had also received the notice to join the war on the border.

With China crossing the border of India's North East Frontier Province in its greed for conquering other countries and arriving at the threshold of Tezpur, all courageous Indians were called to stop eating curry and make China cease from seizing the city.

The clarion call also reached Harshabardhan in Calcutta. But he said, 'No, I shall not go to war.'

'What are you saying, Dada?' Gobardhan was speechless in surprise. 'Didn't you go to England to fight in the war? And now that the war has come to your own country are you going to turn down the opportunity?'

'England? That was Spain,' said Harshabardhan. 'I fought in Spain.'

'Same thing. Spain is on the way to England. You fashioned the defeat of Hitler's Fascists there, didn't you? I fought too, right next to you. That wretch retched our story in his book.'

'Which wretch?'

'Your pet, that Chakarbarty, of course. As if you don't know him.'

'Why shouldn't I know him. I've read the book. He gave me a copy too. He exaggerates a lot, though. Does he take drugs, do you think?'

'Yes, he drags it out too much, all his lies are lying around in the story.'

'You could say he knows the lie of the land. But that's not the point. The point is, are we going to have to go to war all our lives? When I was young I fought, but don't you suppose I'm not as strong at this age as I was once? I'd fall if I even tried to lift a gun. And then there's the parade? I'm too old to be going on long marches.'

'And it's not March either, it's peak summer,' agreed Gobardhan.

'Exactly. Let the young men fight. We'll read about it in the newspapers. Or I'll tell that Chakarbarty to write some stories about the war . . . we can read them in his book.'

'That's true.'

'And they're the ones who're fighting now anyway. The jawans.'

'Jawans. Who are they, Dada?'

'Hindi word. Jawan. Brave. So brave they can die just like that.'

'Like you,' Gobardhan informed him.

'Me, die just like that? Meaning what? 'Harshabardhan was astonished.

'That's what Boudi said the other day,' revealed Gobra.

'Your Boudi said I can die just like that? She's the one who will be the death of me. Did she say this to a military officer?'

'No no. To that Chakarborty.'

'Tell me everything. If he goes and writes a story and publishes it, I've had it. There's already this notice to deal with it.'

'You remember Boudi's holy ritual of Itu-pujo ? When she was done with the rituals she told me, go get a Brahmin, will you? I have to offer a meal to a Brahmin. Off I went to Chakarborty. When he heard about the feast he got dressed to leave at once. But when I told him Boudi was planning to feed a Brahmin as part of her religious vows, he had second thoughts. "I'm not exactly a Brahmin, you see," he said. "I don't even have the holy thread." "Have you sent it to the laundry," I asked. "Not exactly," he answered. "I don't quite remember going through the ceremony." "Maybe you didn't, but your father did, didn't he?" I asked. "Even if you aren't a Brahmin yourself, being the son of one is enough." So he came for the feast.

After he had stuffed himself, he belched and said, "That was quite a spread, Boudi. Superb cooking. Just one item missing. No sea-fish. You could have made some." Boudi said, "Do you suppose anything unadulterated is available these days, Chakarborty moshai? All we get is rice with cankers, rotting vegetables, everything cooked in groundnut oil. Bound to make you see something fishy in your plate anyway. So I didn't make any sea-fish." At this the man jumped. "What! Are you saying this meal will be hard to digest? Do you have any digestive medicine? I need some."

"All we have here by way of a digestive . . ." Boudi said ". . . is Gobra's brother. He can die just like that. Though he's asleep now."'

'The things your Boudi says! If I can still fight, then who's what they refer to as a vet . . . vet . . . what's the word? It's on the tip of my tongue. Who's a vet . . .?

'Veterinary?'

'Vet . . . a former soldier. But your Boudi's certificate will force me to go to Tezpur, it seems. I'll be widowed at this age.'

'You will be widowed? What do you mean?' Gobra's mouth fell open.

'Not me . . . your Boudi. She'll become a widow. Same thing. And then she'll see what happens. She won't be allowed any fish, and her favourite cat will run away without fish. Let's see how she copes.'

'Let Boudi cope with her problems. We have to cope with ours first,' said Gobra.

'Nothing to cope with,' his brother answered. 'Didn't I tell you this will force me to go to Tezpur? The head rolling on one side, the body on another.'

'I'll roll next to you, Dada,' Gobra said, unable to contain his excitement.

'How awful,' Harshabardhan moaned pitifully. 'Our family will become extinct. A thousand sons and grandsons more, a family killed by blood and gore.' Confusing himself with the Lankan massacre in the Ramayana, he was overcome by Ravana's grief.'

'You're mourning in vain, Dada! You have neither sons nor grandsons,' said Gobardhan. 'How can your family become extinct?'

'You're a grandson of our father too. If you become extinct, so will our family.' Harshabardhan's grief overflowed. 'Our illustrious family line will disappear. It won't grow anymore. Whether it's gunfire or gun-fear that kills it, it's the same thing.'

'No, never. You don't think they'll send you to the fr . . . the fr . . . fr . . .'

'What are you toing and froing for?'

'Fron . . .' Gobardhan was speechless.

'Meaning?' Harshabardhan sounded annoyed.

'They're unlikely to send you to the front.' Gobardhan had finally found the word he was looking for. 'You're supposed to have won the war in Spain. They must have read it in the book. That's why they've summoned you. They're bound to make you a general. You won't have to fight in the trenches or die from enemy fire. You'll find it easy to escape from the back room.'

'Easy! There's no escape, the God of Death is donning his cape. You have no idea what war is like.' Harshabardhan sighed. 'The hardest place is the end, where friend can never meet friend.'

'But brother will meet brother,' assured Gobardhan. 'I'll stay close to you, I won't run away.'

'Don't bother me, brother. Now read to me what the notice says.'

'There's an address on Gokhale Road,' Gobra said. 'The recruiting office. We have to present ourselves at 10 a.m. the day after tomorrow and register. They will enroll us after a medical examination.'

'And if we don't go?'

'Someone will come with a warrant to arrest us.'

'And if we run away?'

'They'll put out a summons. Probably put the police on our trail.'

'Police! Oh my god!' Harshabardhan said in panic. 'Then there's no question of not going. We'll go.'

On the appointed day, the brothers appeared at the recruiting office as directed, standing next to each other. Harshabardhan was the first to be examined.

'Name?'

'Harshabardhan.'

'Age?'

'Forty-two.'

'Father's name?'

'Poundrobardhan. Mother's name . . .'

'No need. Address?'

'Chetla.'

'Profession?'

'Timber merchant.'

'Do you consider joining the Indian Army an act of great value, of glory?'

'Of course, of course.'

'Which division of the armed forces would you like to enlist in?'

'I beg your pardon?' Harshabardhan did not understand the question.

'There are several divisions, you see. Infantry division, armoured division, airborne division . . .'

'I want to be a general straightaway,' Harshabardhan informed him.

'Are you mad?' The recruiting officer couldn't help asking.

'Is that a precondition?' Harshabardhan enquired. 'Must I be mad before I can be a general?'

Without answering, the officer turned to Gobardhan.

'Name?'

'Gobardhan.'

'Age?'

'Thirty-five. Ditto ditto ditto for the rest.'

'Meaning?'

'Meaning – the address, father's name, and profession are all the same as above,' Gobra explained. 'We're brothers, you see.'

'I see. Very well, go into the next room for your medical check-up,' said the officer. 'Only if you pass your medical exams will you be enlisted.'

'We're safe now, Dada,' Gobardhan whispered on the way. 'When we've never passed a single exam in our lives, how are we supposed to pass the medical exam now? We're bound to fail. We've been saved.'

'Don't be sure of their felling us.' Harshabardhan wasn't convinced. 'Nothing is to be felled in wartime, nobody's a useless fellow.'

The doctor took one look at Harshabardhan's enormous paunch and rejected him. 'No, impossible.' Harshabardhan was about to protest that he had seen many generals with paunches like punching bags, although only in photographs. But the doctor dismissed his protests with a couple of strokes on his belly.

It was Gobardhan's turn next. Having passed all the exams, he had to have his eyes tested.

'You can read the letters on the chart, can't you? The chart on the wall.'

'What! You mean there's a wall there?'

'Your eyesight doesn't seem very good.' Holding up a huge aluminium tray two feet from his eyes, the doctor said, 'What am I holding here?'

'An eight-anna coin, isn't it? Or is it a four-anna coin?'

Gobardhan was also rejected on grounds of poor eyesight.

Coming out of the recruiting office on Gokhale Street, the brothers heaved a sigh of relief. 'Come Dada, let's give ourselves a treat,' suggested Gobardhan. 'It's almost 2.30. Let's have lunch somewhere and watch a matinee.'

It was past 3 p.m. by the time they had eaten their way through the menu. They entered the theatre in the darkness, taking the seats assigned to them.

When the lights came on at the intermission, Harshabardhan jumped out of his skin. The doctor who had checked Gobardhan's eyes was sitting next to him. Here he was, comfortably watching a film despite his poor vision. Gobra was bound to be caught now.

Harshabardhan nudged his brother with his elbow to point the doctor out.

Gobra wasn't daunted, however. Instead, he turned to the doctor and said, 'Excuse me, madam, this IS bus no. 33, isn't it?'

'What?' The doctor was startled by this unexpected interrogation.

'I mean, pardon me, madam. This bus IS going to Chetla, right? It's all very well to have pushed through the crowd to get in, but am I even on the right bus? Will I get to Chetla?'

3

Harshabardhan Hunts a Tiger

Harshabardhan could no longer be contained. He grew desperate to kill a tiger.

'Another minute and it would have killed me,' he said. 'I'm not going to spare that blasted tiger.'

"What'll you do with a tiger, Dada? Not keep it as a pet, by any chance?'

'I'll kill it. It killed me, and you expect me to let it go?'

'But it hasn't killed you. Couldn't.'

'I had a narrow escape. Would any of you have been able to save me if it had killed me.

Gobardhan was silent, unable to answer this.

'This moustache saved me, so to speak.' Twirling the two ends of his moustache, Harshabardhan said, 'It's only thanks to this moustache that I'm alive. Or else I'd have met that other man's fate . . .'

He pointed to the corpse. 'If you leave my moustache out, that clean-shaven man is nobody but me. An exact replica of myself. It could have been me instead of him. I had a close shave.'

Gobra couldn't answer this either.

'Ei Chowkidar!' Harshabardhan roared suddenly. 'Can you get me a gun? I'll pay whatever I have to.'

'What will you do with a gun, Babu?'

'Hunt the tiger, of course. What does a man want a gun for?' He turned to me. 'You'll have to write a story about my valour. All those stories you've written about me are a load of nonsense. People read them and laugh. I've been told everyone laughs at me.'

'So what? I shall write the story of your hunt. This very tale of how you shot a tiger. But why go to so much trouble and try to kill a tiger with a gun? Why even venture into the forest, for that matter? Shooting a tiger doesn't need so much effort. You don't even need a gun. Any make-believe tale will do. Any cock and bull story. The pen is powerful enough to kill a tiger with a cock and a bull.'

'Catch a tiger by its tale?' Gobra quipped.

'Did you say you were ready to pay, Babu?' The chowkidar had been deep in thought all this while, but finally he spoke. 'If you give me some money I can get you a gun for a day or two. I can get the inspector's gun, in fact. If I tell him that we're being troubled by a tiger which must be killed, he will lend it to me at once. I'll return it afterwards.'

'What will I do with just the gun? He'd better provide bullets and cartridges too. I can't beat the tiger to death with the gun, can I? If I try something like that, the tiger will finish me off first.'

'Of course he will give cartridges too.'

'Then go and get them quickly. Don't make me wait. I'm not budging till I've killed the tiger. I shan't even have a glass of water today.'

'Bring back some food along with the gun,' advised Gobardhan.

'You can't shoot a tiger on an empty stomach,' I said. 'Even if you don't have any food, you must have a little ganja at least.'

'Should I get some?' asked the chowkidar.

I said, 'If there's ganja who needs a gun? Who needs to risk one's life in the jungle, for that matter? No need to carry a gun around, one can kill tigers without leaving home.'

'Forget it, we don't need ganja or anything,' declared Gobardhan. 'Babu's joking with you. Get some bread and butter and biscuits and chocolate if you can.'

When the gun arrived, Harshabardhan asked me, 'Do you know how to shoot a tiger?'

'Yes, if it pauses before attacking. But usually it gets its paws on you instead.'

'You have to go deep into the jungle, Babu,' the chowkidar informed us.

But the first creature that came forward to welcome us when we stepped into the depths of the forest was neither a tiger nor a tiger-cub, but a bullfrog.

This pleased Harshabardhan enormously. 'This is a good omen,' he announced. 'Frogs are auspicious, did you know that, Gobra?'

'Goddess Lakshmi's mount?'

'No, that's the owl,' said Harshabardhan. 'Everyone knows that.'

'You're right,' I agreed with him. 'It's owl the oily people whoo give a whit for wealth, don't you know?'

'Then is the frog the mount of Ganesha . . . but no,' Gobra corrected himself, 'that's the rat.'

'I didn't say it's auspicious because it's anyone's mount. I'm speaking from my own experience. Don't you remember what happened when we first came to Calcutta, Gobra? How I found a wallet on the road in Dharmatalla?'

'I remember. You hid it in your pocket so that no one could see it. And then when you took it out of your pocket when we came home . . .'

'. . . I found it had four legs. A wallet with four legs? When I examined it properly, what I found was that it was a frog flattened under the wheels of a tram.'

'And you simply couldn't get anything out of the wallet.'

'That's true, but our luck turned immediately afterwards. Our timber business made us rich. We came here to blow up money, but we were swamped by the money we made instead.'

'Then the frog must be Vishwakarma's mount,' Gobardhan hazarded a guess. 'He's the god of workers of the world. Always banging away with a hammer.'

'If not a bang, definitely the bank. The bank is the support of the world's workers. In which case it's the World Bank that's Vishwakarma's mount.'

'Same thing.' Harshabardhan was elated. 'He's always banging while I'm always banking.'

'That reminds me of a story,' I said. 'The tale of the hopping frog. By Mark Twain. I read it as a child.'

'What does Mark Twain mean?' asked Harshabardhan.

'The name of a writer. American.'

'And the hopping frog?'

'Obviously, the frog who hops about.'

'Hopping against hop, you mean?'

'You could say so. I certainly hoped the story would be funny, though I don't know whether the frog was hopping mad. Listen to the story now. In Mark Twain's time people used to bet on frog-racing like they do nowadays on horses. The frog who could leap ahead of the rest won the race. So, to prevent the other frogs from leaping, what some people would do was to feed them stone chips on the sly.'

'And the frogs ate those stone chips?'

'Silly creatures, you see. Ate whatever they were offered.'

'I don't believe it,' Harshabardhan shook his head.

'Why not examine it for ourselves?' said Gobra. 'Here's a frog, let's find out whether it will eat stones or not.'

Gobra got hold of some gravel and tried to make the frog swallow them. And, how strange, the frog became obedient at once, swallowing them one by one. When he had eaten several, his stomach swelled. And the frog sat placidly, its head lowered. Far from hopping about, it had no strength to move.

'You're right, it did eat them. But can it digest them?' said Harshabardhan.

'You bet. We digested so much stone at his age Dada,' Gobardhan reminded his brother. 'If you consider all the gravel we swallowed with our rice, we must have eaten a smallish mountain by now. And we digested it didn't we?'

'Of course,' I said. 'Or you'd be dying by now, and not in jest either.'

'Dada! Look!' Gobra screamed in terror.

We looked. A gigantic snake, possibly a cobra, was winding towards us.

'Don't move an inch,' the chowkidar warned us. 'If you do, the snake will bite. Not you, its target is the frog.'

He was right, we observed, standing motionless. Without even bothering to give us a glance, the snake appropriated the frog. Grabbing the frog in its mouth in an instant, it proceeded to swallow the creature slowly.

We watched the amazing ingestion. The plump frog travelled along the snake's throat and towards its lower half, getting stuck at one point. No matter how hard the snake tried, it could not push the frog further down. The amphibian remained like a hump on its back.

The snake had obviously not had a hunch that the frog would make it hunch-backed. Its face was transformed. As though it had lost all interest in life. With a disconcerted expression, it settled down like a mass of flesh, disillusioned with the world.

It did not display any enthusiasm for anything thereafter.

'The snake has bitten off more than it can chew, Dada,' said Gobardhan. 'There's a frog in its stomach, and stones in the frog's stomach. First the frog has to digest the stones. Only then can the snake digest the frog. I doubt if they can do it in this lifetime.'

'We'll see which of them digests the other,' I said. 'Why don't we get our digestive systems going meanwhile. Shall we have something to eat?'

Spreading a newspaper on the ground, we sat down to our meal of bread and butter. Not too far from the snake, who was coiled up like a marble right next to us.

Suddenly we heard a rustling sound from the other side of the jungle.

'The tiger has arrived, Babu,' the chowkidar exclaimed. We looked up to discover the tiger was indeed there, waiting in the undergrowth to pounce on us.'

'Looks like the bread and butter will become the tiger's meal after all,' I said regretfully.

'But how? We've polished it all off, we haven't left anything for him,' said Gobra, popping the last slice of bread into his mouth.'

'In the same way that the stones have become the snake's meal,' I elaborated.

'I'll kill him with one shot. Just a minute.' With this declaration Harshabardhan picked up what he thought was his gun. The next moment he jumped sky-high. 'Oh my god, this is the snake. Where's the gun?'

'I've got the gun, Babu,' said the chowkidar. 'You never took it from me. I've been carrying it all this while.'

'Do you know how to fire a gun?'

'No need, Babu. If the tiger comes towards me I'll smash his head with the butt of the rifle. Don't panic.'

Meanwhile Harshabardhan had whirled the snake in his hand thrice in the air and flung it at the tiger.

The snake struck the tiger with a great deal of force.

But even before that could happen, while the snake was spinning in the air, the frog shot out of its mouth at high speed, and all the stone chips in the frog's stomach were ejected like bullets towards the tiger, hitting it on his head.

And under this unexpected blow, the tiger fainted and slumped motionless to the ground.

'Did the tiger die of snakebite?' We approached the unconscious beast.

Without wasting a moment, the chowkidar flattened the tiger's head with the butt of his gun. 'It was the impact of your snake that killed the tiger, Babu. Still, better safe than sorry, so I used the gun too.'

'Now what?' I asked. 'If only there was someone to take a photograph, we could have posed with the gun with our feet planted on the tiger.'

'Where will we get a photographer in the forest, Babu? I'm going to present the tiger to the inspector. I'll get a reward, I might be promoted from chowkidar to dafadar at once for killing the tiger. I'll be a sergeant.'

'Dada makes a duffer out of the tiger and you get promoted to dafadar, with both sir and gent in your rank,' observed Gobra. 'How odd.'

'So you did manage to kill the tiger with a bullfrog before the gun could be cocked. A real cock-and-bull story,' I told Harshabardhan admiringly.

4

Harshabardhan Goes on a Holiday

In Darjeeling, the brothers felt desirous of riding horses. So they purchased a pair, one for each.

'Horse-riding is excellent exercise, Dada, did you know?' said Gobra.

'Of course I do. But the problem is that both the horses are of the same size.'

'We bought them for exercise. Not same size.'

'Not talking of exercise. They're the same size – meaning identical. Same height, same width, in length and in breadth – absolutely indistinguishable. That's what I'm talking about.'

'Thank goodness.' Gobra breathed a sigh of relief.

'There have to be degrees in everything, or else how will we tell them apart? Great-greater-greatest, for instance. Or tall-taller-tallest . . .'

'For example?' Gobardhan was eager for actual evidence.

'For instance, you are tall – five feet four inches. I am taller. And the Himalayas are the tallest.'

'I see.'

'There are no degrees between these two horses. So I'm wondering how to tell your horse apart from mine. Your horse is used to carrying your light weight – if I were to climb on it by mistake, it might collapse out of sheer lack of practice and not get up again. Carrying my weight might end its wait to get to heaven.'

'That's worrying.' Gobardhan looked worried. 'Even if my horse doesn't die beneath your bulk, it might go lame. And lame horses keep putting their hooves into potholes and tripping. My horse might stumble and grumble.'

'It's bound to. What can I do?' His brother was unable to provide any comfort. 'It's no use crying ourselves hoarse over the horses now.'

'I have an idea, let me cut off my horse's tail.' Gobra came up with a suggestion. 'You'll be able to tell my horse apart from yours then.'

Fetching a pair of scissors, Gobra cut his horse's tail in half. 'You wanted degrees. Here's your answer.'

'Since you've scissored your horse's tail, let me seize mine.' Twirling his horse's tail, Harshabardhan tied a prominent knot in it. 'If yours is smarter, mine is smartest.'

They praised each other's ponytails effusively.

The brothers were enjoying the breeze during their ride, swapping tales about barbers, when Harshabardhan's horse lost half its tail to a length of barbed wire.

'Now look what's happened,' Harshabardhan told his brother. 'We can no longer tell them apart by their tails.'

'So I see,' answered Gobra. 'I'll just trim my horse's mane then. There's no other option.'

With its hair trimmed, the horse looked rather handsome. Most modern.

Giving it an admiring glance, Harshabardhan said, 'Your horse is very civil, I see. You've trimmed both head and tail and yet it's not complaining. What an ass.'

'I'm warning you not to call my horse an ass,' Gobra protested. 'I just gave it a shave to save it from death in case you try to ride it by mistake.'

'Well done. Now I can say neigh to myself before jumping on your horse,' said Harshabardhan.

There was another accident the next day, while the brothers were riding side by side. Harshabardhan was drawing luxuriantly on a cigar when Gobra wrinkled his nose. 'Your cigar is so long, Dada, and what a foul smell.'

'Hmm, I can smell it too. They needn't have such a strong odour just because I ordered them specially.' Harshabardhan pointed with his nose at the tobacconist. And his eye fell on his horse's neck. Oh no, the sparks from the lighted cigar had landed on the horse's mane, burning them. The neck was almost bare now.

'Now the sparks have burnt my horse's mane too. It looks just like yours. We can't tell them apart anymore.'

'What to d1o, then?'

'What can we do? Don't blame me if I jump on your horse by mistake and it misses its footing under my weight.'

'This is trouble!' Gobra considered the danger to his horse a danger to himself too.

What was he to do now? He had no answer. Should he cut one of the ears of his horse, while his brother's . . . should be cut both the ears of his brother's horse? But what if the horses didn't want to be earmarked for this treatment and galloped away? What then?

After much thought he finally came up with an idea. 'Have you noticed that your horse is white, Dada?'

'So I see.'

'And mine is black. See?'

'Yes, I do.'

'Then yours is white and mine is black – can't we remember this black-and-white truth, Dada?'

5

Harshabardhan Kicks the Bucket

Eventually the day came. That final tragic day dawned even in Harshabardhan's life.

He suddenly began to gasp during a conversation with me. 'I have a strange feeling in my chest,' he said. 'A pain of some sort.' He lay down flat.

It was obvious. The first news that strikes one on unfolding the newspaper – there's always one such news article every day – it would clearly be read in tomorrow's paper too.

What was about to happen right now usually led to the sort of news that made me feel the pain of losing not my wife but my life. Thanks to high blood pressure, my heart was at risk too. News that made my heart flutter and convinced me it was I who had died, forcing me to spend a comatose half hour in bed.

He hadn't been well for some time, with a pain on the left side of his chest. Because of the pressure of work and the resultant lack of time, he hadn't been to a doctor despite meaning to. And now he was about to slip beyond a doctor's care – the ever-lethal coronary thrombosis was knocking on the door of his heart.

Still, it was necessary to send for a doctor.

I took a taxi to rush to Dr Ram. He was the only renowned doctor hereabouts.

When I told him what happened, he turned sullen. Without a word he took an ampoule out of his famous doctor's bag and filled his syringe.

Scared, I told him, 'No, not me. Nothing wrong with me. I'm not ill. Please don't give me an injection. It's Harshabardhan-babu's chest . . .' I retreated several steps in fear. This was Dr Ram's disease. Whenever anyone appeared in his presence to tell him about illness, he poked him or her with his syringe.

He climbed into the taxi without responding, still holding the syringe. When he got out, it was still in his hand, though he had transferred his doctor's bag to mine.

When I entered, Harshabardhan was supine on the bed. It was obvious he was done for. He had expired.

Passing the syringe to me with the words, 'hold this,' Dr Ram examined Harshabardhan's pulse. Then he placed his stethoscope on the patient's chest. Finally, he announced grimly, 'It's all over.'

I was still standing with the syringe in my hand, like a doctor's compounder out of his element.

'Pass the syringe,' he commanded, looking at me. 'I won't waste the medicine. Since it was meant for him, let me give him the injection instead of wasting it.'

Like plunging a knife into a dead man, he stabbed the departed soul's chest with his syringe before counting his fee and re-entering the taxi with his bag in his hand.

Harshabardhan's wife proceeded to flop down on the floor and wail. I covered the corpse with a white sheet.

Wiping his tears, Gobardhan said, 'There will be time for tears. First, the last rites for my brother. I'm off to New Market to get flowers. The cot in which we'll take him to the crematorium

has to be decorated. Get the devotional singers if you can – do your duty as a friend.'

'But we need the death certificate first,' I informed him. 'Else they won't let us enter the crematorium with the corpse. The doctor was in such a hurry he forgot. He left without issuing the death certificate. Let me get him to make it out. On the way back, I'll check about your devotional singers.'

I got the certificate but not the singers. No one knew where they lived. All I could find out was that they were in great demand these days. There was a virtual epidemic of deaths everywhere among well-fed, wealthy people.

But I was startled as soon as I returned with the death certificate. The wails had turned into screams.

Entering, I discovered Harshabardhan's wife was also lying lifeless.

'Such a pious wife, she has chosen to die along with her husband.' I touched her feet in deference and then moved my fingers beneath her nose – but what's this! She was breathing! Merely unconscious, then.

She sat up when I splashed water on her face.

'Why did you scream? What's the matter?' I asked.

She pointed to Harshabardhan in terror. 'He seemed to be moving.' She couldn't keep herself from expressing her anxiety. 'Dying on a Saturday! What if something's got hold of him? What if he's turned into a ghost, or spirit, or something like that?'

'Are you asking if he's turned into a spectre? How could that be possible? A philanthropic, pure soul like him must have gone directly to heaven. He cannot possibly become a ghost – nor can he be possessed by one.' But although I offered words of courage, my heart was trembling. 'Just chant Lord Rama's name, everything will be fine.'

'I can't. It's my father-in-law's name,' she said. 'You'd better do it instead.'

'No need. Ram is part of my name, as you know. On top of which I have Dr Ram's certificate – here you are. No ghost can come anywhere near me.'

At this moment Harshabardhan stirred and sat up in his bed. He looked around in wonder for a few moments and then said, pinching himself several times, 'No, I'm clearly alive.' Then he asked me, 'Why the glum face, Shibram-babu?' To his wife, he said, 'Why are you weeping, my dear?'

When none of us answered, he continued, virtually asking himself, 'Did something happen to me?'

Assuming that the question was meant for me, I countered with my own question. 'You should tell us whether something happened to you.'

'Nothing at all,' he told us. 'It was like a very bad dream. That's how it feels now.'

'In that case nothing is wrong. Don't worry about it anymore,' I told Harshabardhan's wife. 'Why not make your husband a cup of coffee?'

She brought two cups of coffee, one of them for me.

Draining his cup, Harshabardhan said, 'What's the piece of paper in your hand?'

Turning it over in his hands, he said, 'If only one could make sense of doctors' prescriptions. Only compounders can decipher them.'

Meanwhile, Gobra arrived with several bunches of flowers.

'What are all these flowers for? What's the occasion?' Harshabardhan asked in surprise.

'Don't you remember it's your wedding anniversary? I had sent Gobardhan to the market for flowers. It's a new flower-bedecked wedding night for you.'

'Anniversary? Today? I'd completely forgotten.' He muttered to himself, 'I never remember. I don't want to, either. It's not my wedding anniversary, it's the day of my sudden death.'

I threw a sharp sideways glance at Harshabardhan's wife. She didn't say anything. Her serious expression seemed to have grown graver.

Handing Dr Ram's certificate to Gobra, Harshabardhan said, 'Go to the dispensary across the road, Gobra, and tell the compounder to make this medicine quickly for me.'

When Gobra had left, he turned to me and said, 'I had such a strange dream while I was asleep. I'll tell you about it some time. You'll get a story out of it. Not that I was particularly surprised by the dream, because you always dream when you're asleep. But what I'm wondering about is why I feel asleep at this unusual hour. I don't usually sleep this way at this time. That's what surprises me.'

'There's no fixed hour for sleep.' I was forced to trot out excuses for sleep. 'Anytime is bedtime. The night, obviously, but you can sleep whenever you want to. I always sleep whenever possible. At unusual hours, in fact. There's no tax on sleep, after all . . .'

Gobardhan returned with a bottle even as I was speaking. 'The compounder's made this mixture. To be taken at three-hour intervals. Have a dose at once.'

Swallowing his first dose, Harshabardhan felt a little revived. 'Wonderful medicine. Made me feel better at once. Leave the prescription with me.' Taking the death certificate from Gobardhan, he tucked it under his pillow. 'I feel like I've been given a new life. Must continue the medicine. Dr Ram's prescription, after all. This medicine answers when you call out to it.'

'It's thanks to your destiny of not being widowed that he survived this time,' I whispered into Harshabardhan's wife's ears, making her smile. With her husband hale and hearty, I left their house.

A few days later, just as Harshabardhan was passing Dr Ram's house, it began to rain. He took shelter near the front door. When he found himself getting drenched, he decided to meet the doctor and thank him for prescribing such effective medicine for his recovery.

As soon as he entered the doctor's chamber, the doctor began to shriek.

'Don't you recognize me, doctor? I'm Harshabardhan.' Quickly he added, 'I've been very well ever since I began to take your medicine. The pain in my chest is gone too. That's what I came to tell you.'

'But I didn't prescribe any medicine. I only gave you a corvine injection. Then was it in reaction to the injection that you came back from death . . .'

'What! You didn't give me this prescription, then?' Harshabardhan interrupted him. 'I've been carrying this piece of paper next to my heart. I am never parted from it. It's the medicine you prescribed here that gave me a new lease of life.'

He held the piece of paper out for Dr Ram.

'Prescription? Let me see! Hmm . . . this is your death certificate, which I issued.'

'Death certificate! What?' It was Harshabardhan's turn to jump out of his skin. Trembling, he sat down on the chair.

'My death certificate? You're right.' He controlled himself and continued. 'Then that's what it was. Now I understand the significance of that horrible dream I had . . . finally.'

'You haven't died, then? Or are you a ghost?' Although he felt a stab of fear, the doctor decided this wasn't terrifying. 'Look, the late Mr Harshabardhan, it's not my fault. I didn't kill you.

I didn't get the opportunity, so to speak. You were done for before I arrived . . .'

'Oh, I'm not blaming you. It's true that I died. For which I am responsible. There's no error in my death certificate. I was even taken to the court of the God of Death. Let me tell you what happened, then. You'll be astonished to hear how I came back from the land of the dead.'

Although his suspicions had not quite been dispelled, the doctor was all ears.

'The messengers of death marched me off the court of the God of Death,' Harshabardhan continued, getting into the spirit of things. 'He was seated on a throne behind an enormous register. The keeper of his records sat in front of him. Although no one pointed him out to me, it was easy to recognize him at once. The messengers of death stood in small groups.

When he saw me, the God of Death told his keeper of records, "Check his tally of good and bad deeds, will you?"

When he had been through the books, the keeper said, "His good deeds are in the majority, my lord. But he has committed a few sins too."

"What sins?"

"Adulteration. Which almost everyone in India indulges in these days."

"What did he adulterate?"

"Timber."

"But my Lord! Is timber food or medicine? Why should I adulterate it then?" I couldn't help protesting. "Do people eat wood? Have you ever heard of adulterated wood? Is it even possible?"

"But he did it," said the keeper of records. "He would pass off deadwood as rare teak."

"You surprise me, Mr Accountant," I said. "There's no such thing as a deadwood tree. Where's the question of passing off deadwood as teak, then? If you were talking of redwood, it might still have made sense."

"By deadwood I am referring to shoddy quality," the keeper of records explained. "You sold cheap wood, claiming it was expensive."

I had to accept this. "Yes, my lord, I did. But our scriptures say that you must follow in the footsteps of great men. That is just what I have done. Is there one great man today who does not adulterate recklessly? So, I decided to also . . ."

The God of Death interrupted me. "How long should this man be sentenced to hell, accountant?"

"My lord! A minimum of twenty years. A score. That will be enough to even the score. And his time in heaven will be much longer."

The God of Death looked at me. "Would you like to do your spell in hell at the beginning or at the end?"

"Whatever you decree," I answered, my palms joined in deference. Instead of answering, he began to examine his nails carefully. I noticed that he had grown them a lot – had he started from scratch?

"You need to cut your nails at once, sir," I told him. "They really are far too long. If you allow me, and if I am given a razor, failing which a blade, I can cut them for you."

"Not my nails. I was trying to nail down the situation which is prevalent in your Calcutta."

"I have no situations which are prevalent, sir, but I have a witch which is prevalent. The person who occupies my house is best described as a witch. I haven't come across another married woman who's such a shrew, a bigger nag, or more quarrelsome. I have to live with a witch . . ."

"What if we were to let you live and send you back home?"

"For god's sake, sir, I'll die. Again. I don't want to go back to a wife like her, I'd rather go to hell."

"So I can see. But the situation outside your home is even worse than the one in your home. The roads are full of potholes and garbage from everywhere. People are packed into the trams and buses like sardines, and the roads are choked by processions. There are strikes in every office, grit in every plate of rice, contamination in all food, sand in sugar, mud in sand, water in milk. In trying to nail down Calcutta I seem to have nailed down hell. What was it you had said, accountant? Twenty years in hell, wasn't it? Your lifespan is being increased by twenty years. Go and raise hell in your city."'

'And at once I came back to life,' said Harshabardhan, sighing deeply.

6

Harshabardhan Sees the Sun Rise

It would probably be more accurate to say the sun was devoured, not viewed.

After the original Rahu, only Hanuman had succeeded in grabbing the sun and hiding it away, but no matter how much he might flex his muscle, Harshabardhan was no Hanuman.

So when he said, 'I'll see what Uncle Sun can do,' my mouth fell open in surprise, to tell the truth.

Without responding to my gaping mouth, he posed a second riddle. 'We hunted a tiger in the Sunderbans, now let's go after the tiger in the hill.'

'As far as I know,' I couldn't keep myself from saying, 'there aren't too many tigers in the hills. They're more likely to be found in forests. Elephants live in the mountains. Haven't you noticed how elephantine the mountains are?'

'Who told you that?' he protested. 'Why do they call it Tiger Hill then? Haven't you heard of Tiger Hill?'

'Of course I have. But as far as I know, there are no tigers on that hill. It's a place for tourists.'

'The sun rises on that hill every morning. Apparently it's a beautiful sight.'

'That's what people go there to see.'

'So shall we. You, Gobra and I. The three of us.'

It was evening when we reached Darjeeling. We found a hotel near Tiger Hill.

After all the arrangements had been made, we told the hotel-owner, 'Please wake us up very early tomorrow morning.'

'But why?'

'We are masters of sleep, you see . . .'

'You could call us mountains of sleep too,' said Harshabardhan. 'Like the mountain of Ghoom which we crossed on our way here. Ghoom means sleep, doesn't it? So don't expect us to wake up easily.'

'We cannot wake up on our own,' added Gobra. 'That's why we're requesting you to . . .'

'May I ask why?'

'Why? We have come all the way from Calcutta just to see the sunrise.'

'To see the sunrise? Are you telling me you can't see it in Calcutta? Doesn't the sun rise there?'

'Of course it does, but catching a glimpse is another matter. There are such high buildings everywhere that there is no way of knowing when the sun has risen or set.'

'And besides, there are no tall trees in Calcutta that we could climb for a view . . .' Gobra always tried to add a tall tale if he at all could.

'No trees, maybe, but no three-storied buildings either? Couldn't you have climbed to the roof?' the manager asked.

'Of course there are three-storied buildings. Multistoried too.' Harshabardhan launched into a detailed description. 'We have houses with twenty floors that will completely floor you. But so what – you cannot see the sunrise even from the terraces of these houses. The eastern sky is hidden behind skyscrapers in the distance.'

'The only way out is to climb to the top of the Shahid Minar . . .' I said.

'But that will take me an entire day. Have you seen how heavy I am?'

The hotel-owner inspected Harshabardhan's bulk on his ardent plea. 'That's true,' he agreed.

'There you are. I'll never get to see a sunrise in this lifetime – being born in human form will be in vain . . .'

'And so we request you earnestly . . .'

'Apparently there is an unrestricted view of the sunrise here, and it seems it is truly a sight to behold . . .'

'Which is why we were telling you to . . .'

'Please wake us up before dawn,' we submitted in unison. 'By force, if needs be.'

'No need,' he informed us. 'There's so much noise here before dawn every day that you will wake up automatically.'

'Why all this noise?'

'Why do you suppose? To catch the sunrise, obviously. No matter what people come here for – for a change of air, or as tourists, or on business – they all have to see the sunrise. They're never satisfied. You could call it an obsession.'

'We're not here for a change of air, or as tourists, or on business. We've come for this very reason . . .'

'That's why all the boarders at the hotel raise such a din before dawn, making so much noise, that we, who work in this hotel, who have to work late into the night before going to bed and don't like waking up early, who have no interest in the sunrise whatsoever even though we exploit the sun for business, who are not remotely bothered, are still forced to get out of bed. We don't wish to disturb any of the boarders, it is not our custom to interrupt anyone's rest . . . but it won't be necessary, because no matter how soundly you sleep, I will be extremely surprised if the commotion at the crack of dawn does not wake you up.'

Relieved, we deposited our luggage in our room, had our afternoon tea, and went out for a walk.

It wasn't the right time for the sunrise, of course, but there were plenty of other sights to see. It was for these exquisite scenes that we went out.

It was almost evening. The hill roads had emptied out. A Bhutia boy was returning home with the cattle he had been tending to, a song on his lips.

Harshabardhan began to express his appreciation loudly.

'Lovely. How melodious. How sweet . . .'

'Such modulation!' Gobra joined in. He was a model of adulation.

'This is Bhatiali music, you know, Gobra. Let it flow into your ears, let it fill your heart.'

'This probably isn't Bhatiali,' I protested mildly. 'The boatmen of East Bengal sing Bhatiali songs as they row their boats in midstream. It's named after bhati, the Bangla word for low tide.'

'Then this must be a qaw-wali,' Harshabardhan said knowledgeably.

'How is that possible? If the boy had been herding cows, it might have been, but he looks after sheep.'

'Not the qaw-wali either?' Harshabardhan seemed disappointed.

'You could call it Shepali music, Dada. The boy can be called a shepherd, can't he?'

'You could call it the child of folk music.' I wouldn't play second fiddle to anyone when it came to researching music. Just the way the cat turns into a tiger in the forest. 'This child too will become someone important when he grows up. As soon as he grows a moustache this song can be effortlessly termed a major hit. Right now it's in a minor key.'

As the boy with the sheep approached us, singing, Harshabardhan began to rummage in his pocket. 'Let's give him a tip. Oh! I've left my wallet at the hotel. Do you have some money? Or have you left it behind too?'

'Are you mad? I can be parted from my life, but not from my money. Whatever little money I possess is always with me – my pocket is my Reserve Bank. But . . .'

I hesitated. How could I admit of my own accord that Chakrabortys were misers? You shouldn't sing your own praises, after all.

'Then give him a little money. A rupee, at least.'

I did.

The boy was genuinely surprised when he was given the money. He had been singing out of unprovoked happiness in his heart, not for a tip. Still, he was extremely pleased, leaving with his companions after offering us a salute.

Another shepherd boy appeared on the road a little later. Singing the same way, with a flock of sheep in tow. He had to be given a rupee too.

A little later, yet another one. Returning along the same route, singing at the top of his voice.

He was sent on his way with fifty paise, delivered like a cuff on his head, so that we could get some respite from his fusillade of notes.

Then began a real avalanche of singing shepherd boys on the road we had taken . . . and I began to get rid of them one by one. Three of them got fifty paise each, and the next four, twenty-five. Because of my dwindling resources, I had to send the rest on their way with small change.

'It's not the same boy every time, is it, Dada?' asked Gobra suspiciously. 'Maybe he just wants to get more money out of is.'

'Do you think it's the same boy?' Harshabardhan asked me.

'How should I know? It's difficult for me to tell one Bhutia boy apart from another. It's equally impossible to separate one flock of sheep from another. All sheep look the same to me. Identical.'

'Really?' Harshabardhan was astonished.

'Oh yes, all of the same variety. Identical in appearance and in the sounds they make – whether it's the sheep or whether it's these boys.'

'Let's climb that mound there and see where the boy goes.

We clambered on to the hillock.

Just as we'd suspected. The boy was indeed circling back around the hillock, his voice blaring as he approached us. But this time he no longer ran into us. And as a result, he stopped circling and went on his way. And we were finally free of his circle of conspiracy.

But the boy had left me penniless. A little more of his singing and my ears would have been ringing. He had managed to damage several of the membranes already, only my brain was still intact. Like me, he had bankrupted my hearing too.

Only years of self-defence had saved my ears from destruction.

After feasting our eyes sumptuously on natural beauty and a long walk, it was quite late by the time we returned to our hotel.

Our eyes were heavy with sleep by then, and our legs were trembling. We barely managed to stuff our faces before collapsing on our beds.

'Shut the windows carefully, Gobra,' I told him. 'Or else it might rain anytime.'

'But this isn't the rainy season.'

'You have no idea of Darjeeling's moods, my friend. There aren't too many seasons here. No summer, no spring, no autumn. There are only two seasons. Continuous winter and random monsoon.'

'What do you mean?'

'There are light clouds everywhere, even if they aren't visible. Darjeeling is situated at the same height as clouds, you see. If the clouds find a crack in the window-shutters they will enter the room and it will rain.'

'Really?'

'Absolutely. I can't explain anymore, I'm falling asleep . . .'

'It's all very well to sleep, but keep your eyes open,' bellowed Harshabardhan.

'How can I?' I couldn't help responding. 'I have to close my eyes to sleep.'

'Keep your ears peeled then. Stay alert while you sleep. As soon as you hear a commotion you'll know it's almost dawn. Wake us up then.'

'We'll see,' I said, turning over on my side. Without much hope of seeing too far with my ears.

After a bout of sleep, though, I heard some sounds and sat up in bed. Nudging Gobra, I said, 'Do you hear something, Gobra?'

'Hear what?'

'Sounds like a pakhawaz being played. Someone seems to be signing the raga Bhairav. It's a dawn raga.'

'The sound of a pakhawaz?' Gobra tried to prick up his ears.

Harshabardhan spoke from the depths of his sleep. 'What is it? Is it dawn?'

'I heard some sounds a short while ago,' I told him.

'Is it dawn?'

'So I thought. But I don't hear the commotion anymore.'

'How will you?' said Gobra. 'Dada just woke up, you see. It was his snores you heard.'

'Never. Who says I snore? I never do. I'd have heard if I did, wouldn't I? I'd have woken up.'

'You're as deaf as a doorpost. How will you hear? The nose is so close to the ear, still you can't hear sounds loud enough to bring a dead man to life.'

'You're as mad as a hatter, Gobra. I don't want to waste my time talking to you,' Harshabardhan turned over on his side again – and the rumbling was resumed.

Later, possibly much later, it was Harshabardhan himself who awoke us. 'Do you hear something?'

'Nothing at all,' I said. 'Absolute silence.'

'Isn't it morning yet? Are you serious? Let's open the window . . .' Getting out of bed, he opened the window. 'Good god! It's light already. Come on, get up, rise and shine, quick.'

We jumped out of bed.

'No times to dress. Forget about clothes, we're going for a view, not to be viewed. Just wrap a blanket around yourself. We'll miss the sunrise if we're late.'

Wrapped in blankets, we hurried out.

Tiger Hill was close by. We rushed to the top of the hill.

There was a huge crowd of people. All gathered for a view of the sunrise, no doubt.

'How much longer before the sun rises?' Harshabardhan asked one of them.

'Sunrise?' The man chuckled.

'Not much longer,' I said. 'The sky's clear. There's a radiance everywhere . . . any moment now.'

But the sun just wouldn't rise. 'Why isn't the sun rising?' Harshabardhan was forced to ask someone else.

'Why should the sun rise now?' The man looked at him in surprise.

'I was just saying that the sun should have risen by now. The eastern sky is quite clear. There's sunlight everywhere but no sun.'

'Isn't the sun planning to rise today?' I grumbled.

'The sun is behind that cloud, that's why you can't see it,' the man said. 'As soon as the cloud moves away . . .'

And the cloud drifted away even as he spoke, revealing the sun.

'Oh my god. It's risen a long way already. It's quite late.' Harshabardhan said ruefully. 'We've missed the sunrise.'

'But what's going on?' he screamed suddenly. 'Why's it going down? Why's the sun setting? What's going on?'

'I've never known this to happen.' I was astonished too. 'It's not normal for the sun to break the rules. Does this happen often hereabouts? Does the sun start setting soon after rising – does it forget its way?'

'What do you mean?'

'I mean that we're here to see the sunrise. Even if we couldn't see the sun rise, we weren't unhappy to see it rising, but what's this! It's setting even before it has risen properly!'

'You think the sun will rise in the west for your sake? You've seriously come to see a sunrise at the time of unset?' The man snarled at us.

'Who are these lunatics?' Another person took up the theme.

7

Harshabardhan Versus Gobardhan

Putting the pot on the shelf, Harshabardhan turned to his brother. 'Don't even look this way, all right?'

Gobardhan didn't. His eyes were on his book. He seemed to be devouring the words.

'Why don't you answer? This pot has rashogolla from Baghbazar . . .'

'Fat lot I care,' retorted Gobardhan. 'I know they're booked for you. There may be rashogolla or there may be gold in your pot – what do I care?'

'Don't eat them by mistake,' Harshabardhan told him. 'They're for my afternoon tea. You'll get a few once I've eaten.'

'You can keep your sweets. Your sweetness is all I need.'

'That's true.' His brother was pleased. 'But you must still taste them.'

'I can barely contain my excitement,' said Gobra, turning his lips up along with a page from his book.

'What book are you reading with such close attention?'

'A book.'

'I can see it's a book. Not just one but two, in fact. What's that beneath the pillow? What's its name? Who's the writer?'

'*Cheap Snacks*. The writer's name is . . .'

'*Cheap Snacks*? Look, don't let these rotten books lead to you snacking cheaply on my rashogolla. I won't tolerate these sneaking chaps writing about cheap snacks. And what's that other book in your hand?'

'A story book. *The Danger of Talking*. Same writer. Shibram Chakraborty.'

'Oh dear! You're reading that dangerous man's books?'

'Of course I am? What's wrong with that?'

'Everything! You'll mix up all your words. Sounds and meanings will be confused. You'll look for a twisted sense of everything. Words will command no respect anymore. One word will have multiple meanings, without rhyme or reason. He's pungent.'

'So you think!'

'Let me see the book.' Harshabardhan turned the book over in his hands. 'See, it says here clearly, the perils of talking like Shibram Chakraborty. He's said it himself in as many words. This really is going to be dangerous.'

'If I'm in danger, that's my business. Give my book back to me. Go have your rashogolla.'

'Fine, don't say I didn't warn you. You'll know when you yourself don't understand what you're saying. It's none of my business. By the way, there will be a trunk call from our timber depot in Guwahati. Call me when it comes, all right?'

'All right, all right.' Gobra went back to his book, but he began to wonder. What was a trunk call? From the timber depot. A tree trunk, then? Or an elephant's trunk? Could be a trunk for luggage too. What sort of trunk was this? Musing over all this, he lost himself in his book again.

Taking off his coat, Harshabardhan stretched himself out on his bed, burrowing beneath the blanket. But it wasn't strong enough to keep the cold out. The freezing wind coming in through the door chilled him to his bones.

'Shut the door, will you?' he said, shivering.

Rapt in his book, Gobra was deaf to his pleas.

'Can't you hear?' Harshabardhan was forced to bellow. 'Didn't I tell you to shut the door?'

Gobra was forced to abandon his book. Going up to the door, he put his finger on his lips and said, 'Shhh!'

'Oh god! The disease has affected him already. Did I ask you tell the door to shut up, you idiot? I wanted you to slam the door.'

'Oh, so that's what you meant.' Fetching his brother's expensive teakwood walking stick from the corner, Gobardhan delivered such mighty blows that both his brother and the door screamed in agony. The stick split into three at once.

Seeing Gobardhan reaching for the sandalwood walking stick after destroying the teakwood one, Harshabardhan protested vociferously. 'No need. You don't have to slam the door. You can neither shut the door nor slam it in this lifetime. Anyway, what's done is done. It's all over.' Harshabardhan sighed deeply.

'Why don't you say clearly what you want?' complained Gobardhan. 'The door can't both be shut and slammed at the same time.'

'If only you could understand what I meant. You read the opposite meaning into anything I say.' Suddenly he had a brainwave. If his brother was indeed reading the opposite of what he meant, why not actually say the opposite of what he wanted? That might produce the correct result. 'What I was saying was, open the door. Open it completely.'

'But where's the screwdriver? I'll have to call a carpenter to do that,' said Gobra, sounding unhinged.

This made Harshabardhan sit up and take notice. From his lying position he sat up in his bed and began to ponder over this. He could not fathom how to explain to his brother what he wanted. How could a door be treated? What were his duties towards the door? How could they be discharged properly? How could he get both Gobra and the door under his control in the way he wanted? He couldn't answer any of these questions.

He tried one last time, with the hope that his brother's head wasn't as wooden as the door. 'If I asked you to not to leave the door ajar, would you put several jars by the door?'

'I wouldn't bother. Why should I? I wouldn't give it even a single jar. What does it need jars for? That would be jarring.'

'That's enough.' Harshabardhan shook his head hopelessly. 'No point bothering the door anymore. Can you pour me a hot cup of tea from the thermos flask there? I've been turned into a block of ice.'

'Now this is a very clear request. Nothing to carp about. No carpenter required.' Gobra poured his brother a cup of hot tea and offered it with a smile.

'Ah, what a relief. Another cup, please.'

Gobra brought another cup to Harshabardhan. An empty cup.

'Did I ask for an empty cup?' Harshabardhan asked, as hot under the collar as the tea. 'Didn't I ask for a cup of tea?'

He felt like hurling the cup at Gobardhan hard enough to split his skull, so that he could find out whether his brother's brain had turned to jelly.

'You want tea? You can have more than one tea.' Gobardhan brought half a dozen cups along with the flask, besides three glasses, and held them out to his brother. 'Here you are, pour yourself as much tea as you want and drink it. No one's stopping you.'

He wanted to pore over his book, not pour tea for his brother. Understanding someone who said one thing and meant another was beyond him. A brother was a bother in life. Unbearable.

'Get out of my sight. Don't remain where I can see you.' Harashabardhan proceeded to empty out the flask. 'And where do you think you're going?'

'I'll go downstairs to read my book in peace. You're not going into your office now, are you?'

'Not as long I'm here. That is to say, not as long as you're there.'

'Would you prefer that I died? Would that please you?' Gobra began to sulk. 'Am I not your brother? Weren't we born of the same mother?'

'Did I say that? I meant, not as long as I'm up here, and you're down there.'

'That's neither here nor there. No, it's best to keep my distance from you.'

'Go on then. The further you are from me with those books of yours the better.' Harshabardhan heaved a sigh of relief. 'I only want the best for you. Reading that man's book addles the mind, makes everything confusing. My advice was for your own good, but since you're not interested . . . By the way, you'll be in the office, won't you? Don't forget I'm expecting an important trunk call. Keep your ears peeled for the phone, don't lose yourself entirely in your book.'

Switching the light on in his brother's office, Gobra put his feet up on the table and resumed reading. But it was difficult to keep his mind on the book and his ears on the phone. Even if one could be all ears when listening to a story, how could one read that way? Why not get the trunk-call over and done with right away, wondered Gobra.

He went upstairs a little later to tell his brother, 'Your trunk call, Dada.'

'So soon? How could they get the connection so quickly?'

'I helped get the connection. Through the phone.'

'Very well done. You'd better stay here and read then, while I attend to the call. You don't have to poke your nose into my conversation.'

'I couldn't be bothered,' announced Gobardhan. 'I have just the one nose, and everyone knows it's needed to breathe.'

Harshabardhan could have objected to this with several 'nos', but he ran to answer his trunk call instead.

'Hello? Yes, I had asked for the trunk call . . .' he shouted into the phone. 'Hello . . . hello . . .'

'Ah yes. What kind of trunk do you need?'

'What kind of trunk?' Harshabardhan was a little surprised. 'I had asked for Guwahati. But I'm expecting a trunk from Dilli too. Is this the one from Dilli?'

'Steel trunk? Yes, we have them. What size do you need?'

'Steel trunk? What on earth is that?'

'Yes, steel trunk. If you could let us know how short or long you want it, and the colour . . .'

'The long and short of it is that I don't even know who you are.'

'Our steel trunk shop is in Bentinck Street. We're Calcutta's best-known trunk sellers, surely you know us.'

'To hell with trunks. Who wants your steel trunk?'

'You, of course. You called us on the phone just a few minutes ago. Why don't you try our trunks? You can return them if you don't like them. No one can make them as strong as we do. We can guarantee it. Please do visit our shop. Whatever your preference in trunks might be . . .'

'I don't want to try your trunk. Go to hell!' Harshabardhan threw the receiver back on the cradle and stormed upstairs.

'You . . . you . . . you . . .' he could barely speak in his anger and he finally sputtered at Gobardhan. 'You're a rascal.'

'What's wrong? Didn't you like their trunks? Theirs was the first name among trunk-makers in the phonebook.'

'You . . . get out of my sight. At once. This instant. Else I'll . . . I'll kill you. Get out, you ass. Go wherever you like, you stupid idiot, imbecile, moron. Rush . . . go la . . .'

Before Harshabardhan could complete his angry outburst, Gobardhan jumped to his feet. 'You told me to. It's not my fault. You can't blame me.'

He leapt towards the shelf and grabbed the pot of rashogolla, sinking his teeth into them.

'Rush . . . go la . . . that's what you said. So I'm doing just what you asked me to.' In front of his brother's eyes, which were now round balls of surprise, Gobardhan proceeded to swallow the round balls of sweetness.

8

Till Debt Do Us Part

Let others claim they don't like loans, but I alone will swear by them. I don't think anyone but a moneylender can say they have never borrowed. The road to hell is paved with good intentions. Just like death, debt too is a certainty in life.

If only it was just a matter of a loan, however! But it wasn't. It was my rent that was overdue. That too, not a large sum – only five hundred rupees. But still the landlord appeared in reptilian form one day. 'I've given you enough time, no more excuses . . .'

'Think about it,' I tried to tell him. 'You're pressing me for a mere five hundred rupees. And yet, a lifetime later – after my death, of course – people will point to this house of yours and say, this is where the famous writer so-and-so lived once upon a time.'

'Lived here! Did me a great favour by living here!' The response came like a whiplash. 'Let me tell you something clearly. If I don't get my dues by midnight, then people will say this not a lifetime later but tomorrow.'

The landlord warned me and left. But how was I to find so much money in half a day? No one willingly came near a writer like me in the fear that they would have to lend me money. All writers were 'loanly', and I was a step ahead – everyone knew this.

Should I go to Harshabardhan, I wondered. This paltry amount meant nothing to the brothers. I had made enough money by writing of their exploits, why not exploit them now? They could be good sports and support me.

As soon as I broached the subject, Harshabardhan said, 'Of course, of course! Who's my money for if not you?'

I was startled. It sounded strange.

'You're not such a close friend of ours,' he continued.

'If it's friendship you're talking of . . .' I tried to interrupt.

'Yes, I'm talking of friendship. You're not our friend, after all. We're told not to lend money to our friends. For that's the end of both the money and the friendship. Of course, if it's the kind of friend you'd rather be rid of, the only way to ensure that is by lending him money. You'll be free for life.'

Oh! If only I belonged to this second category of friends! I sighed.

'But you're not a friend, Mr Writer. Writers can never be anyone's friend.'

'No one can be a writer's friend, either,' I said regretfully.

'You have no liabilities. What could be better? Since you're neither a friend nor a relative, but only a writer, nothing prevents me from lending money to you. How much do you need?'

'Not much, just five hundred. And I'm not asking you to give it to me for good,' I said. 'It's Wednesday today, I'll return it to you on Saturday.'

I gave him my word. There was no other way to secure a reprieve from the landlord, but I had to give Harshabardhan my word. I gave it without much thought – but on Saturday morning it became a source of concern.

I was walking along the road, lost in thought and at my wits' end, when I ran into Gobardhan.

'Will you honour a request of mine, Gobardhan?'

'What request?'

'I'll tell you only if you promise not to tell your brother.'

'Why should I tell Dada, it's not as though I tell him everything.'

'The thing is, can you lend me five hundred rupees for a few days? It's Saturday today. I'll give it back to you by Wednesday evening.'

'Is that all?' Without any further ado Gobardhan took five one-hundred rupee notes out of his pocket and gave them to me.

I went directly to Harshabardhan.

'Have I kept my word or not? I may be an impoverished writer who plays with words, but I never go back on mine.'

Harshabardhan accepted the money in silence.

'You had probably expected your money to be lost forever. You had probably assumed I would never pass this way again in my life. You thought . . .'

'No, I never even imagined anything like that. I had completely forgotten about the money,' he declared. 'Believe me, I wasn't even remotely worried when I lent you the money, but I am worried now that you've returned it.'

'You must have assumed that I'm returning these five hundred rupees to build my credibility so that I can borrow a thousand next time,' I said. 'And that I will even return the thousand and borrow two thousand. Then, when I have taken the amount up to nine or ten thousand, I won't come within a thousand feet of you. Isn't this what you're thinking? Isn't this what you're worried about?'

I probed his psychology. Perhaps mine too.

Resorting to 'eyecology', he looked at me piercingly and said, 'No, that's not what I was thinking. I was wondering how you managed to return the money so soon. How could your need have been met so quickly? Never mind, don't hesitate to ask if you need money again.'

Needless to say, I nodded mentally. Writers were always in a hazy state, they never hesitated to ask for anything.

The need for money arose again as early as Wednesday. I had to borrow from Harshabardhan to pay Gobardhan back.

'Well, Gobardhan? I kept my word, didn't I? Here's your money – returned with gratitude.'

Soon I had to go back to Gobardhan. 'I said I'd pay you back on Wednesday and I did, didn't I? Have I ever failed to keep my word?'

'Why are you saying all this?' Gobardhan couldn't understand my preamble.

'I need some money again. Five hundred rupees, just like last time. That's what I've come to you for. I'll return it next Wednesday, I promise.'

In this way, Harshabardhan and Gobardhan, Gobardhan and Harshabardhan – my dates with debt were kept every Saturday and Wednesday. But one day, I ran into both of them together.

Walking side by side, they stopped on seeing me. Their eyes were questioning.

Maybe the look signified nothing but casual curiosity – was I well, or, where was I going. But because of my guilty conscience, their eyes only appeared to hold a demand.

'Harshabardhan-babu, Gobardhan, I'm going to say something, please don't mind . . .' I began. 'Gobardhan, you must give five hundred rupees to Harshabardhan every Wednesday. And Harshabardhan-babu, you must give five hundred rupees to your brother Gobardhan every Saturday. Wednesdays for you, Gobardhan, and Saturdays for you, Harshabardhan-babu. You won't forget, will you?'

'What's all this?' Harshabardhan was flabbergasted. 'I don't understand at all.'

'What it is is that I want to settle this once and for all. I don't want to be a middleman between the two of you.'

9

Harshabardhan and the Illusionist

Man rules supreme – nothing can be truer. But everyone knows that the supreme ruler up there is unshakeable. So, how long can a man retain his supremacy? Sooner or later he is bound to be in a soup.

We had always thought of Harshabardhan as being second to none, but I had never imagined that he could voluntarily pick the second spot. Though it did take more than a few seconds.

It was his wife who corrected my mistake, giving me the news angrily as soon as I arrived. 'He used to be quite sharp all this time, but he's lost his edge ever since he started keeping your company. No brains anymore.'

'But I'm the one who's blunt,' I pretended to protest mildly. 'I always ask bluntly for money, while his edge comes from the money he already has.'

'Never edge up to sharp people,' quipped Gobra. 'The sharp edges are blunted by friction. That's what's happened to Dada.'

Finally I found out the entire story. How the sleight of hand was performed right in front of Harshabardhan's eyes. The car had vanished virtually under a magician's wand.

It all began with Harshabardhan going to the nearby saloon for a haircut. The saloon was very crowded yesterday morning, forcing him to wait for some time.

The owner brought Harshabardhan some books. 'No need to be bored, sir. Leaf through these magazines. Three other people are waiting, it'll be your turn after them.'

As he was turning the pages, a stranger came up and sat down next to him.

'Namashkar, Harshabardhan-babu.'

'Namash-car.' Although Harshabardhan echoed the greeting, he had no idea who the man was.

'You don't know me. I'm practically your neighbour – I live a couple of lanes away. But I know you very well. You're a pillar of our society. Is there anyone who doesn't know you?'

'Oh no, I'm just an ordinary man.' Harshabardhan was disconcerted by this fulsome praise from a stranger.

'You are not only not ordinary, you are extraordinary. Do you know that all of us in the locality – old and young, master and servant – follow in your footsteps?' The man gave an example. 'For instance, I followed you into the saloon to get a shave, though I usually shave myself at home.'

'I'm here for a haircut.' Harshabardhan tried to dismiss him. He didn't care for being held up as an example.

Holding the books out to the man, he said, 'They've given me these books to read. It will take some time to get a haircut or a shave. As you can see, no one's free. Read these in the meantime.'

'These are thrillers,' said the man, wrinkling his nose. 'Ghost stories. Makes your hair stand on end. Why do they keep such trash in the saloon?'

'That's exactly why,' answered Harshabardhan. 'It probably helps the barbers if your hair stands on end.'

He appeared cheerful at arriving at this thrilling solution to a deep mystery.

'You're right,' agreed his companion. 'This is the only decent saloon in the neighbourhood. But then who could be bothered to come all this way to the main road every day just for a shave. I happened to be passing this way when I saw you, which is why . . . where did you park your car?'

'Car? I don't have a car!' Harshabardhan ran his finger over this stubble. 'It's because I don't have a car that there's so much trouble at home. My wife nags me every single day. I can't get hold of a car.'

'What! You of all people can't get hold of a car?' The man was flabbergasted.

'It's been three years since I applied. But finally there's a ray of hope. Eventually my name's risen to the top of the list. I saw my name ahead of everyone else's. Just the other day. I think I'll get my car now.'

'Well you might,' the man assured him. 'Being on the top of the list always helps.'

'Yes, the agent said the same thing. Your car's arrived, he said – it will be released in a day or two. You can pay for the car and take it home, he said.'

'You're a fortunate man,' said the main in elation. 'What car is it?'

'A Fiat, he said,' answered Harshabardhan. 'A Fiat, or some such name.'

'F . . . I . . . A . . . T.' The man seemed deflated suddenly. 'A Fiat.'

'What kind of car is it?' Harshabardhan was keen to know.

'A terrible car. You could call it Fear instead of Fiat.'

'What do you mean?'

'Fear. Terror. A very bad car.'

'But the agent said it's a very good car.'

'They always say that. Their commission comes from sales, after all. Fat profits.'

'Really?'

'You've got a big car, haven't you? Is it a big Fiat or a baby Fiat?'

'No, not very big, said the agent. But not too small either. Medium-sized.'

'How many people will use it?'

'Three of us. My wife, my brother Gobra and myself. Add the driver and that makes it four.'

'It'll be fine for you then.'

'Yes it will. Gobra can sit next to the driver – nothing wrong with that. My wife and I can sit at the back. Both of us are a bit on the portly side, but the back seat will support us.'

'Your wife and you may be together though thick or thin,' the man seemed to be weighing his words, 'but first the car must move.'

'Why, are you saying the car won't move?'

'Why not? Of course it will. It just has to be given a push. You have to be pushy. How many of you in the car did you say? Not counting the driver, of course, because he will be at the steering wheel. How many of you again?'

'My brother, my wife, me, and a servant – that's four of us, more or less.'

'Certainly the car will move if four of you push it,' the man said confidently. 'With the force of four you could even make an elephant move.'

'But why will it have to be pushed? It's a car, not a cart.' Harshabardhan was surprised.

'Only at the beginning. Once the engine starts working the car will roll smoothly. These models don't have good accelerators, you see. These cars are not self-starters. That's why they're often shelved.'

'Why should a new car be in this condition?' Harshabardhan was astonished.

'You don't think they send new cars to India, do you? All second-hand cars,' the man informed him. 'In fact, who knows how many hands the car has actually passed through? But they pass them off as brand new here.'

'Is that so? I had no idea!' Harshabardhan appeared crestfallen. 'Their showroom had a couple of those Fiats. Someone showed me one of them – absolutely new. It looked terrific, I must admit.'

'Only on the surface,' the man smiled knowingly. 'Beneath the veneer it's battered goods.' Pausing for breath, he continued with fresh verve, 'Besides, these cars have another flaw. They consume too much petrol. Gluttons for fuel.'

'That's all right. We like gluttons. We're gluttons ourselves.'

'Not just fuel, they're full of other problems too. They stutter.'

'Stutter?' Harshabardhan couldn't utter a word.

'The car skids without warning.'

'Runs over kids without warning? Is that what you're saying?'

'Kids?'

'Kids. Baby goats. Bid a man to go the kid. I'm well-read.'

Harshabardhan had no hesitation in candidly confessing that his education was limited to baby goats.

'No, not kids. I'm taking about skidding. Sliding across the road without warning. And killing people in the process sometimes.'

'What!' Harshabardhan recoiled in horror.

'It's a dangerous car, I tell you.'

'Oh god!'

'The brakes are bad, you see. You'll find out for yourself. You'll go bankrupt paying compensation for the people whom it will kill. Not even a lakh will compensate for the lack of safety in this car.'

'Lakhs will be lost over the car?'

'The brakes will make you broke,' concluded the man.

Harshabardhan seemed to have a breakdown.

'And it's all over if you have a collision. Bump against another car or even a lamp post and your car will be finished. It's very fragile.'

'We'll be finished too, won't we?'

'Definitely injured if not dead. You'd better insure both the car as well as yourselves. Nothing to worry about in that case. You'll get compensation for both.'

'What's the use of being compensated after death?' Harshabardhan didn't seem convinced. 'Even if we don't die, merely lose a limb or two, such a loss can't be compensated by monetary profit.'

'That's a matter of perspective. Some people spend their entire lives earning money. Some let their money flow like water to save their lives. To each according to his taste.'

'I'd have been in trouble. That car would have killed me. Thank goodness I met you today, you've saved my life. And my money, too.'

'Not at all. Don't worry. Cars are not for travelling. For that you have taxis. What could be better than getting a taxi as soon you step on the road? And it's much cheaper too. Do you suppose a car like this one is easy to maintain? Fragile, rotten parts, falling apart. It will spend half its days at the workshop. Even after it's repaired, it will be back to square one in a day or two.'

'I don't want such a car. I shan't take it.'

'Why not? Didn't I say cars are not for travelling in? Cars are decorative pieces for the home, to lift its status. A car parked outside the house raises your worth to neighbours.'

'My wife says the same thing. We're being shamed in the neighbourhood because we don't have a car, she says.'

'She's right. What's a home or a car for if not to be shown off to people? So that the neighbours turn green with jealousy. But this car can't exactly be shown off. If you really want the neighbours to see it, you have to run over them. Brushing past them or spattering mud on their clothes would have been enough, but this car cannot do all that. It won't even start, leave alone splash them. But yes, you can make your neighbours hear it.'

'Hear it? What do you mean?'

'Slam-bang, of course. You can do that. Slam-bang.'

'Slam-bang?'

'Yes. Didn't you say there were four of you? The car will be parked in your portico, won't it? Each of you must stand at one of the doors. And then slam-bang.'

'What is this slam-bang business?' Harshabardhan was irked by the repeated reference.

'Each of you should open the door and then shut it. Hour after hour. A series of slam-bangs. The neighbours will get an earful of your car. You can drive it home all day.'

'But is that a good idea, slamming and banging constantly?'

'Then intersperse the slam-bang with honk-honk. Blow your own horn every now and then.'

'To hell with all the slam-bang. I'm off to cancel my order – I don't want a car that needs slamming and banging.'

Harshabardhan shot out like an arrow, without waiting for his haircut. Cancelling his order for the car, he went back home.

'No, my dear. I cannot cope with all this slam-bang.'

When he explained everything to his wife, she raised the roof at once, sparing no pain to explain to her husband that his stupidity was beyond measurement.

Smarting under his wife's rebukes, he went back sullenly to the agent this morning. 'I want the car. I've changed my mind.'

'What car? When you cancelled your order, the person who was at No. 2 got the car. There he is, he's just taken delivery of the car.' He pointed to the owner of the car. 'But if you like I can keep your name at No. 2. You'll get the next car. Maybe another three hours or so.'

The car drove off, blowing its horn, under Harshabardhan's nose. All he could say was, 'It's that man. The slam-bang man from the saloon.'

Mentally, Harshabardhan slam-banged his head against this second person singular.

10

Harshabardhan is Deceived

Harshabardhan sent for Gobardhan as soon as he came back home. 'I just met a scou boyt.'

'Scou boyt? What on earth is that?'

'You don't even know who a scou boyt is? Those who help others.'

'Scou bout! Such a strange name!' Gobardhan said in astonishment. 'What does it mean?'

'Mean? The meaning's not particularly difficult. It's exactly what the words mean. A scou is, of course, a cow, and boyt! Boyt refers to . . .

Gobardhan joined the search for meaning. 'It doesn't mean boisterous by any chance, does it?'

'Boisterous? A boisterous cow? What do you mean?' Harshabardhan was rather surprised. 'How can a cow be boisterous?'

'Meaning cows that have gone to the dogs,' Gobardhan explained. 'Who are beyond redemption.'

'That's all very well,' said Harshabardhan, 'but it wasn't a cow, it was a little boy. We were on the same tram. Dressed in khaki shorts and shirts, with a handkerchief round his neck, out to do his good deeds. But I didn't realize he was a scou boyt.

How could I? All I knew was that a little boy was sitting next to me. I found out a little later, when I escaped death by the skin of my teeth. Another moment and I'd have been beneath the tram. It was the scou boyt who saved me. It's a rule that they have to help others, you see.'

'Wonderful! What a useful boy! Not at all like others of his age.'

'Absolutely. So I've decided to become a scou boyt too. I'll help everyone I meet, everyone I see. I'll insist on it. What do you think?'

'Scou boyts have a uniform. Do you have one?'

'No, uniforms are too uniform for me. I don't have to be a typical scou boyt to help people, do I? Can't I force them to accept my help? What's wrong with that?'

Harshabardhan was reminded of his vow when he woke up the next morning.

'Yes, today. Today, not tomorrow. I'm going to start helping other people from today onwards. Being unemployed won't work. I will do something or the other for someone or another if I get the opportunity. I must, or else my life will be in vain.'

Suddenly it occurred to Harshabardhan that charity could well begin at home. Why not start with Gobardhan? He could easily consider his brother an other and try his hand at helping him.

And then? Then there were always the brothers of the others. He could help them at leisure.

So Harshabardhan began with his own. 'Gobra! Gobra my brother! Gobra, where are you, you wretched fool?'

How strange! Here he was, chasing the object of his altruism, but there was no sign of the beneficiary. Just imagine!

Gobra appeared at the house. 'Why the urgent summons so early in the morning?'

'I was wondering whether I should do you a favour,' announced Harshabardhan in his baritone. 'What do you think, good idea?'

'Me! Do me a favour? What favour?' Gobra was baffled. 'Why me?' He was apprehensive, too.

'It's essential. You won't understand. Go get a piece of wood. At once!'

'Whatever for?' Gobra was even more astonished.

'I'll show you, just go get one.' Harshabardhan bared his unbearable burden. 'You'll see for yourself.'

Grabbing the piece of wood, Harshabardhan said, 'Suppose I carried you around on my back today onwards, wouldn't it be of great help to you?'

'Me? On your back? Why on your back?'

'Then you won't have to put any effort into moving about. How you must suffer from having to walk. What's wrong with getting someone to carry you around on his back?'

Gobardhan tried to digest this. 'I can't say. It might be fun.'

'That's what I'm thinking of doing. I'll carry you everywhere on my back. You'll be backing me all the time. Just like back-seat driving, my back will be your seat for you to drive me. All right?'

Not even the prospect of such control could tempt Gobardhan, who disagreed, saying, 'Do you really think that's a good idea?'

'Why not? It'll be a favour for you, it'll be good for you, how can it not be a good idea?'

'It's not a bad thing to jump on your back now and then . . . but all the time . . .' Gobardhan's hesitation wouldn't desert him.

'Then there's only one solution. You have to become lame first. It doesn't look right to be carrying about someone whose feet are intact. Doesn't suit him either. It's not really much of a help for him, is it? The truly compassionate is the one who carries a lame man on his back – the real altruist.'

'You're right, Dada,' Gobardhan agreed. 'So you'd better find someone lame and . . .'

'That's what the piece of wood is for. First I'll break your leg so that you can't walk, and then . . .' As soon as Harshabardhan launched himself in Gobardhan's direction, brandishing the piece of wood, Gobardhan appeared to unravel the mystery in some mysterious way. Perturbed by the indescribable possibility of being humiliated, he suddenly leapt to his feet and bounded up the stairs to the room on the roof, bolting himself inside it.

'Hopeless! I can't do anything for anyone in this house. Let me try outside.' Flinging away the piece, Harshabardhan went out, though not before wrapping a handkerchief around his throat. Even if he could not be a full-fledged boy scout, because it was no less difficult to be a boy than to wear a pair of shorts, he did as much as he could. Hence the handkerchief knotted around the neck, as an announcement of his desire for doing good for the world.

By the time Harshabardhan reached the main road, his love for humanity had become stronger. He was salivating at the prospect of salving the pain of the world. He was determined to do something good for someone, anyone, to do it well, at the first opportunity, and disappear afterwards. No one would come to know, it would not be trumpeted in the newspapers. Not for fame, not for profit, just selfless philanthropy for others and for the needy. Even if he could not do much, a little bit at least, even if for only one person.

And why not just one person? One today, another tomorrow. One more the day after. The same way every day. In this way it would become a habit, even a bad habit. This was how people made progress.

Pondering over all this, Harshabardhan leapt into a virtually empty tram. It would go to Galiff Street via Dharmatala. The tram filled with passengers at Esplanade, and Harshabardhan's mind filled with his thoughts.

So many thoughts! Really, it was so difficult to do good for others. Where, when, how to do it? Where were the opportunities?

Suddenly he noticed a young woman sitting close to his own seat, a small baby in her arms. She had a long, thin face; despite her clean clothes, the signs of poverty were evident. It was clear that she was finding it hard to cope with the struggles of life.

Harshabardhan's heart melted at the sight. Here was his chance. A golden opportunity, in fact. A tattered handbag was dangling from the woman's wrist. It was open, observed Harshabardhan.

He could easily drop a rupee or a fifty-paise coin into the bag without being observed. How delighted the young woman would be when she went back home. No, not a rupee, he would slip in a five-rupee note. She would light up at this unknown act of kindness. The very thought sent Harshabardhan into raptures.

Holding a five-rupee note in his hand, he leaned forward casually. His heart thumped at the audacity of this good deed. Just as he was about to let the note drop into her bag, an ear-splitting voice burst through the silence. 'This man is picking your pocket.'

The man on the seat next to Harshabardhan was pointing an agitated finger at him.

Shrieking, the young woman drew her bag to herself. The baby in her arms began to cry. The conductor rang the bell, signalling an emergency. Everyone in the tram turned to stare at Harshabardhan. He withdrew his hand at once, tucked it into his pocket, behaving like a fool.

There was an uproar in the tram, with everyone talking at once. A powerfully built man gripped Harshabardhan's arm without saying a word, and asked calmly, 'Please check whether he's taken anything from your bag.'

The tram stopped. Harshabardhan stammered, 'It's . . . it's not . . . anything like that . . . I . . .'

But how was he to explain that he had been about to do just the opposite of what he was being accused of? Would anyone believe him if he told them that he had been about to put some money into the bag?

'No, he couldn't swipe anything,' the woman grumbled. 'Poor fellow. There were only a few coins in there. They're still there.'

'Do you want to turn him in to the police?' asked the tram-conductor.

'Since he couldn't steal anything, what's the point?'

'Steal? I wasn't stealing,' Harshabardhan said in a strangled voice. 'I . . . I . . . I . . .'

'Shame on you! Trying to pick a woman's pocket. Go hang yourself! Don't we have pockets too? Or do you think our pockets are empty? Throw him out of the tram.' A multitude of voices expressed a multitude of opinions.

The tram was getting late, and the conductor was about to lose his patience. 'Get out,' he urged Harshabardhan.

No appeal against this verdict was tenable. Harshabardhan slunk off.

The adverse outcome of his first attempt at helping others had ruined his mood. It had been a severe blow, and he was a broken, hopeless man. Most of his enthusiasm had evaporated. But when you came to think of it, was not the road for philanthropists always narrow, eternally perilous? Was it not always strewn with thorns? All those saints who had died early, all those noble souls from Jesus Christ onwards who had been killed unceremoniously while trying to help other people – were their histories not the same as Harshabardhan's? His inspiration began to be restored slowly.

Mulling over these things, Harshabardhan walked past Sealdah Station, and eventually found himself out of the city and heading into the countryside. He had undoubtedly walked a long way – several miles, possibly – and was now in a semi-rural place. Yes, this was the sort of place he wanted, the company of the people here was preferable. They were not as suspicious as city-dwellers. They were human, not cynical. Not rotten like misbegotten urbanites. He preferred these people.

And there might be people in need here in this village, someone who needed help at once, who would not object in the least to Harshabardhan's efforts. Someone who would be obliged, who would thank him, who would be forever be grateful, who would consider Harshabardhan charitable instead of a cheat as the city people had labelled him.

Looking around, he saw a peasant's daughter carrying a huge bundle of vegetables on her head – bent over and distressed because of the weight. His earlier determination came back at once. The desire to lighten a fellow human being's load rose in his heart.

Harshabardhan went up to the young woman. Softening his usual baritone as much as possible, he said gently, 'Give me that load, I'll take it home for you.'

Looking at him with suspicion, she said, 'So you're the one. You're that man.'

'Which man?' Harshabardhan became nervous. 'What are you talking about?'

'You're the one who took the basket of *gur* off Pocha's mother and disappeared with it, aren't you? It's not even been a week – have you forgotten already?'

'Me? Why should I have done anything like that?' Harshabardhan was baffled.

'That's what you told her – I'll take it home for you. Just like you told me. We couldn't sleep a wink because of the way she cried all week. And now you're saying, why should I have done anything like that? Why indeed!'

'It wasn't me. Maybe someone who resembles me,' Harshabardhan stammered. 'I've never seen a basket of *gur* in my life.'

'Excuses. You thief! Should I call people? Pocha's mother said the man didn't have a moustache, but now I see you've got one. Fixed one overnight. Trying to fool us! Let me check whether it's real – I'm going to tear it off and give it to Pocha's mother.'

Lowering her load to the ground with ease, the peasant's daughter advanced towards Harshabardhan's moustache with even greater ease.

Harshabardhan didn't remain there another moment. Far from lightening someone else's load, he was about to be dispossessed of his own. Talk about contrary results!

Just as wise men have no qualms about abandoning half their property in times of crisis, Harshabardhan also decided to lower the heavy burden of duty and disappeared, carrying only his own heavy burden.

No, enough of altruism. Hopes of helping others were completely misplaced. He had to abandon all such expectations. Instead of lightening anyone's load, Harshabardhan covered half a mile at lightning speed before breathing a sigh of relief.

He had tried his best, he had used different methods – what more could he do to help other people? He could always save drowning men from death, but there was no one sinking in a river nearby, and he wasn't likely to find anyone like that either.

Even if he did, how would it help? He couldn't swim to save his own life.

Climbing a tall ladder to plunge into the flames in a burning room on the fifth floor of a house and rescuing a little girl would not be an indifferent act of altruism. In fact, it could well be termed excessive. It might not be very difficult for him to keep a ladder handy and then clandestinely set fire to a building. But even if such an opportunity cropped up, he would have to push it aside. He wouldn't be able to touch the ladder lying at his feet. He would be deprived of the honour of performing this good deed – not just deprived, but defrauded. How could he possibly climb a ladder with this bulk of his? Which earthly ladder could support his weight, for that matter? No, it would be astute of him to avoid the desire for performing such good deeds – it was beyond his reach.

No more altruism. He would go back to his staple diet from tomorrow – revert to his usual life. Let the world rot, let people go to hell, he wouldn't lose sleep over them – he would never look back. He was ready to give up his life to help others, but he was unwilling to go beyond that. He would not sacrifice his moustache in any circumstances. His lifespan could be cut, but not his moustache. Even if that meant not going to anyone's help.

11

Brothers in Arms

It was a day for life or death. Bhajahari was being tried at the Sessions Court for murdering his wife. The verdict would be declared today.

Cousins are supposed to look after one another. But Harshabardhan wasn't planning to look in on Bhajahari today.

He had done all the looking after and all the pulling of strings for the case all these days. Not just 100 per cent but 110 per cent. But he wasn't bold enough to go anywhere near the court today. It would be as difficult to listen to a death sentence being pronounced as it would be to watch someone being hanged. Even if he couldn't save Bhaju from death, he might at well save his ears.

He had instructed his brother Gobardhan to phone the lawyer in the bar library during the lunch break and find out the verdict and sentence. But Gobardhan did not have to call, because the lawyer himself passed on the news over the phone. Bhajahari had been given only a life sentence. Which actually meant just twelve years in jail.

'Bhaju's safe this time,' Harshabardhan heaved a sigh of relief. 'At least the poor fellow did not have to hang.'

He sighed again a little later. 'I'm jealous of Bhaju, you know, Gobra.'

'Jealous of what?'

'Once, twelve years ago, I had also been in a murderous mood. I wanted to kill your sister-in-law.'

'What!' Gobardhan recoiled.

'Fed up of her demands, I . . . I . . . don't ask. I thought it would be better to murder her and hang – both of us would be free.'

'You shouldn't even say such things.'

'But I couldn't do it. I'd have been saved. She's wrung me dry over all these years.'

'Are you still planning something like that, Dada?'

'Now? At this age? Impossible. But if only I could have done it then . . .' Harshabardhan lamented his luck. 'I would have been a free man today, twelve years later.'

'Would you have married again after being released from jail?'

'Again? Are you out of your mind?'

'I didn't know you were such a dangerous man, Dada.'

'You bet I'm dangerous. How else would I have brought such danger on myself?'

'Our wonderful sister-in-law . . .' Gobra pulled a long face, saying in short, 'And you . . .'

'She may be a fine sister-in-law, how does that matter to me?' snarled Harshabardhan in response. 'Bhajahari is a very lucky man, he's saved himself from both death and his wife. He will roam free happily in just twelve years.'

'You saved him, Dada,' Gobra declared.

'You could say that. I went to no small trouble to save him – and to save you too.'

'That's true, imagine having to study all over again at this ripe old age. But it was your brilliance that saved Bhaju-da. You're very clever, Dada.'

Although Harshabardhan's chest swelled at the compliment, he had to admit that it was actually Bhaju's own ingenuity that had saved him. As they say, one's own wisdom is auspicious, but a woman's wisdom is suspicious. Had Bhaju's wife been alive and in a position to offer advice, he would not have survived.

Harshabardhan had rushed to meet Bhajahari on hearing of his imprisonment. 'I'll put top lawyers on the case, Bhaju, don't worry,' he had assured his cousin.

'Fat lot the lawyers can do.' Bhajahari didn't have much faith in them. 'All they'll say is, let them find you guilty now, we'll get you out on appeal.'

'What do we do then? Get the witnesses to lie?'

'That does work, but there's no scope for that here. I surrendered on my own with the blood-smeared axe after the murder. I confessed everything.'

'So the same axe has handled both of you.'

'Do you suppose I was in my senses? You have to save me. I don't mind life imprisonment, but please make sure I don't hang . . .'

'I have all the money in the world,' Harshabardhan told him. 'I won't pinch pennies . . .'

'When I'm out of jail I'll find a wife after my heart and settle down again.'

'You can never find a wife after your heart. You have to mould yourself after her heart. Just like I have moulded myself.'

'Listen, Harsha, this case won't be settled in the lower court. If you can bribe the jury in the sessions court . . .'

'Say no more,' Harshabardhan interrupted him. 'If anyone hears they will put me inside too. You have to go to jail even for paying bribes. Don't worry. I assure you that everything that can be done with money will be done.'

At the sessions court, though, Harshabardhan found that it would be a difficult proposition. The jury comprised grand people with grim expressions, whom he would not be able to influence.

Still, he recognized one of them. An impoverished schoolmaster from his own neighbourhood. He had to accept a salary of forty rupees while writing a receipt for a hundred and twenty, and had to give ten private tuitions from dawn till dusk to earn another fifty and support his parents.

Harshabardhan decided to concentrate on him.

He brought it up with Gobra. 'We have to win him over by getting him a private tuition that pays a couple of hundred.'

'But whom will he teach? You don't have a son for him to give lessons to,' Gobra pointed out.

'That's true.' Harshabardhan surveyed his household mentally and found that by way of another male there was Gobra, and by way of a girl or woman, his wife. He didn't dare tell her to study, for that might lead to her becoming a widow after she had murdered him. Therefore . . .

'There's always you. A younger brother is just like a son. Haven't you heard it said that an elder brother is like a father? You will study.'

'Me?' Gobra was dumbfounded. 'At this age?'

'There's no fixed age for education. You have to pursue knowledge all the time. People learn till they die.'

'No Dada, I'm not up to studying now.'

'But you're not actually going to study. Only pretend to.'

'I can't pretend. I'm terrified of schoolmasters. They'll make me kneel down on the bench.'

'That's true, they will,' Harshabardhan was compelled to agree. 'But I can replace the benches with a soft mattress. It won't hurt your knee so much.'

'So what? It'll hurt my self-esteem, won't it? What if he boxes my ears?'

Harshabardhan had to resort to emotion. 'But Gobra my brother, who will care for a Bengali if not another Bengali? Who said this?'

'Chandrashekhar.'

'Chandrashekhar said this?' Harshabardhan was astonished.

'No. Kapalkundala.'

'Kapalkundala said this?'

'Then it was in *The Poison Tree*. Yes, *The Poison Tree*, I'm positive.'

'The Poison Tree! Do trees talk?'

'Bankim Chandra, then.'

'You're right. It was indeed Bankim Chandra. Think about it. And here it's not just about another Bengali, it's about someone even dearer. A matter of life and death. Who will care for a Bengali cousin if not a Bengali cousin?'

And so Gobardhan had to become a student in middle age. Someone who had not even passed Class Six would now have to take his school final exam. His first lessons with the teacher were in arithmetic.

That too, involving the problems in Chapter 37. 'Explain this sum to me, sir.'

The teacher did.

'Now explain the sums in Chapter 38.'

'Do the sums in Chapter 37 first and show me.'

'Why bother, sir? I've understood them.'

'Prove that you have by doing them.'

'Are you suggesting I haven't understood them? What are you saying! What have you been explaining to me all this while?'

And so they ploughed through the chapters by the day. The load of sums kept increasing. Eventually Gobra couldn't take it any longer and pleaded with his brother. 'I can't cope, Dada. He keeps asking me to do sums. Save me.' So Harshabardhan shouldered his brother's burden himself.

And added a sweetener, in the form of one hundred hundred-rupee notes. Handing half of them over to the schoolmaster, he said – 'The rest are yours too. I'll give them to you later.' Then he proceeded to teach the teacher a new chapter of arithmetic.

'There's not much you have to do – just bring the other five members of the jury round to your viewpoint. Which you can. Everyone admires teachers – they respect them and fear them too. This will be an easy task for you. You can teach these old boys the same way you teach young boys in your class – that's all.'

'You're saying I have to ensure somehow that he goes to jail, right? That his punishment shouldn't be anything but jail. Very well, I'll try my best. Let's see.'

'Clearly Mastermoshai did quite well,' Harshbardhan told Gobardhan. 'He has managed to save Bhaju from the gallows. And you deserve praise for this too, Gobra. It was only possible because you made so many sacrifices to study.'

Even as they were speaking the schoolmaster appeared, a smile of achievement on his face.

'Come in, Mastermoshai, do come in.' Harshabardhan greeted him effusively. 'We salute you. We'll never be able to pay back our debt to you.'

After the schoolteacher had taken a seat, Harshabardhan pulled the bundle of notes out of his drawer and handed them over. 'Here's your remaining five thousand. Our modest offering. Not that this is sufficient to compensate for your noble assistance.'

'No, please don't say that. Gratitude is priceless. How many people can offer it?' The schoolmaster added, 'I'm no less gratified for having managed to keep my word, Harshabardhan-babu.'

'It must have been very difficult to persuade the jury.'

'Difficult is putting it mildly. I've never faced a more insurmountable challenge. You know what the problem was?

The other members of the jury are all married, and fed up of their nagging wives. Bhajahari-babu was a hero to them. They felt he had committed no crime in killing his wife. They want to do the same thing themselves, but cannot, while Bhajahari-babu did. He was a valiant figure in their eyes.'

'Is that why they wanted him to die like a warrior on the gallows?'

'Not exactly. But then I don't understand the significance of having a wife, since I have never married. I can barely support myself on my meagre salary, leave alone a wife. I realized that I would have to devise a plan whereby the baby was thrown out but not the bathwater. It was very difficult to convert the sentence to life imprisonment, you know. My speech to them lasted nearly three hours – only after that could I get them round to my viewpoint.'

'Or else they would certainly have pronounced the death sentence,' Gobardhan observed.

'No. They wanted to exonerate him honourably.'

12

You Think it is Easy to Bell the Cat?

It's true that I cannot defeat the great soul Kumbhakarna when it comes to sleep. He used to sleep for six months at a time. But I run him a close second – I sleep the entire night at a stretch.

Not even a robbery can interrupt my snores. I've even observed on waking up in the morning that an earthquake had visited during the night, but there had been no disruption in my sleep. The houses nearby had collapsed, the neighbours had panicked, but nothing could come between me and my sleep.

But even this uninterruptible sleep of mine was disturbed one midnight. I sat up with a start in bed.

Bram-babu . . . Bram-babu . . . Bram-babu . . . I could hear a continuous wail at my door. As though it would break the door open.

Bram-babu? Who on earth was Bram-babu? Whose name and fame did it signify? No one with that name lived here. Then what was this pounding loud enough to wake the dead?

Rubbing my eyes as I opened the door, I discovered Gobardhan Chandar standing outside.

'Oh, it's Gobra. But why at this hour? Why were you screaming as though you've been robbed? What's the matter?'

'It's amazing how you can sleep. You beat even Boudi hands down. I've been screaming at the top of my voice for such a long time. My voice cracked, but there was not a crack in your wall of sleep.'

'That's all very well, but why Bram? That's not my name, it's Shibram.' I was more upset at my name being fractured than at being woken up. 'Where's my Shi? My Shi?'

'I have never seen your she. You don't have a wife. I've only see the he in you. Hee hee.' He sniggered. 'I've seen Itu-di and Bini-di here sometimes, but neither is your she. They're like your sisters, Bram-babu.'

When I heard him Bramming me to my face again, I felt like slamming the door on his face. Instead, I controlled myself and said, 'Fine, but what's the matter?'

'Dada told me to run to you, so I came running.'

'Because . . .?'

'Because Boudi was sleeping with her mouth open, you see. A rat's got into her throat . . .'

'What! My goodness!' I said in alarm. 'Is it stuck in her throat? Did you pull it out by the tail?'

'There's no tail sticking out or anything, how are we supposed to pull it out?' said Gobra. 'It's not stuck in her throat.'

'Not stuck? Thank goodness.' I breathed a sigh of relief.

'It's gone all the way in.' Gobardhan explained. 'Burrowed into her stomach.'

'Oh dear! What is she doing now?'

'Nothing. Sleeping as peacefully as before. She probably doesn't even know there's a rat in her belly. Amazing how she sleeps.'

'Yes, quite extraordinary,' I had to admit. 'This is what you call the sleep of the virtuous. Deeper even than mine. This is probably what they call beauty sleep.'

'I have no idea whether it's beauty sleep or duty sleep, but Dada is at his wits' end. Will Dr Ram be available at this time of night? Will he pay a visit even if we pay four times his fee?'

'He might. We have to try.'

'That's why Dada sent me to you. In case you can persuade him . . .'

'Let's try our luck.'

We arrived in front of Dr Ram's house. 'Let go another of those,' I told Gobardhan, 'like the one you let go at my door. I have no idea how deep Ram-babu's sleep is.'

'Let go what?'

'A sound like a battering ram. Or a hammering on the door. Whichever you prefer. It's a ramshackle door.'

Without waiting for me to ram my point home, Gobra let out a rambunctious yell. 'Tor-babu . . . Tor-babu . . . Tor-babu . . .'

Gobra had undocked the doc.

'Just because I asked you to let go, you didn't have to let the doc go from the doctor,' I interrupted. 'The doctor may think you're tormenting him with your Tor-babu cries.'

'But you told me to. That's why I cut the doc off . . .' said Gobra in surprise.

Doctors are light sleepers by nature. Maybe waiting for a call makes them callous about sleep. Soon the doctor peeped out of from the first-floor balcony. 'Who's there?'

'Us. Here to fetch you,' Gobra informed him.

'Who's the patient?' he asked.

'Not us, sir,' I told him. 'We're extremely impatient.'

'Who's ill?'

'No, no pills yet,' I answered, because that was what I thought he had asked. 'This is Gobra. Brother of Harshabardhan . . .'

'Who?'

'You don't know Harshabardhan, sir? Not a harsh man, though. And this is his brother . . .'

'Can't understand a word of what you're saying. Wait, I'm coming downstairs.'

The doctor opened the door to his chamber and we went in. Gobra explained about his sister-in-law in detail.

'What is your sister-in-law doing now?'

'Sleeping soundly, with her mouth open. Just like she was earlier.'

'She's sleeping with her mouth open? Then just hold a mousetrap near her open mouth, with a few flour balls in it. The rat will come out on its own.'

'That it might, but how will I find a mousetrap at this hour of the night? We don't have one at home.'

'In that case dangle a piece of bread from a string in front of her mouth. As soon as the rat smells the bread . . . I don't see any other way out. If it won't come forth on its own . . .' the doctor came forth on his own now. 'You know my fees are fourfold at night, don't you?'

'We do. We'll pay.'

'Very well, I'll be there in a few minutes. I need a little time to get ready. Go dangle the piece of bread near her nostrils meanwhile. As soon as the scent of the bread spreads through her breath, the rat will pop out. Maybe even before I'm there.'

'I'll do that. But please come. My brother won't be reassured till you're there.' Gobra rushed off, telling me to escort the doctor.

When the doctor and I arrived, Harshabardhan was waving a fat tilapia fish near his wife's mouth. A living tilapia.

The fish was wriggling, but still he kept waving it. While his wife went on sleeping.

'Where on earth did you get a living tilapia at this hour?' I asked in astonishment. 'The markets must be closed.'

'We keep tilapias in our tank,' he told me. 'My wife loves them, you see.'

'But I asked you to dangle a piece of bread.' The doctor was even more astonished than I was. 'Why did you replace the bread with fish? Do you suppose rats are attracted by the smell of fish?'

'Then let me tell you what happened, sir,' began Harshabardhan. 'My wife was sleeping with her mouth open, all right? As she does every day. Very bad habit. But then who dares shut his wife's mouth? When she's asleep her mouth's open and when she's awake her mouth doesn't stop . . .'

'I know, I know. I'm fully aware of wives who mouth off,' the doctor broke in. 'But I had said . . .'

'Listen to me first,' Harshabardhan stopped him. 'You know rats emerge from their holes, don't you? And that they also hole up in those same holes?'

'Everyone knows that,' I interjected.

'Now you've seen how wide my wife opens her mouth. Mosquitoes and flies can get in easily, so when a rat gets a chance . . . .'

'I know, I know. I've been told the rat found an opening and wedged itself in.' The doctor grew testy.

'And I sent Gobra to fetch you as soon as the rat went in. But soon after he left, what happened was . . .' Harshabardhan looked thrilled. 'How was I to know that a cat was waiting to pounce on the rat? It was lying in ambush, and gave chase as soon as it saw the rat. And rats always retreat into their holes when frightened. So when it saw my wife with her mouth open, it may have thought this was its hole and . . .'

'. . . run into it. Everyone knows. Never mind all this. Come to the point.' The doctor tried to shorten the preamble.

'The cat chased the rat into my wife's stomach.'

'What!' The doctor was astounded. 'An entire cat in her stomach and she didn't even realize? Still asleep? How is it possible?'

'That's how she sleeps. I doubt if she'd have woken up even if it had been an elephant instead of a cat.'

'Why didn't you pull the cat out by its tail at once?'

'I tried, but there was nothing to be seen. No tail. Everything inside. Nothing sticking out of the throat. So when Gobra told me about the bread, I said, no point worrying about the rat now, we need to get the cat out. Go get me a tilapia from the tank.' Like playing the almighty to god, Harshabardhan explained his reasons for doctoring the doctor's orders. 'That's why I'm waving this fish near her mouth. I only modified your prescription . . . if the cat emerges, it will be with the rat in its mouth, after all.'

'Let me check the condition of the patient.' Dr Ram pulled out his stethoscope. 'I've never had a patient like this. A patently new and nasty illness.' He contorted his face.

The stethoscope is meant for the chest, isn't it? But instead of the chest, the doctor placed it on Harshabardhan's wife's stomach. I was surprised. The doctor's examination of her belly set off alarm bells in my mind.

Was he muddled by her middle? Wasn't he wasting his time at her waist? 'Why are you examining her stomach?' I couldn't help ask. At once I added, 'How is her heart?' to change the subject and make him realize his mistake.

'I'm not checking her heart. I'm checking the heart of the matter,' the doctor responded. 'I don't hear a peep from the cat. Not even a meow.'

'Can you hear the rat?' I asked.

'Will a rat dare make a sound in the presence of a cat?' Gobra was surprised at my question. 'Does it have the courage to talk when being stalked?'

'And do you suppose it's still in this lady's stomach?' responded the doctor. 'It's long gone into the cat's stomach. That's why I was only trying hear the meow.'

'You think that's easy?' I said. 'Belling the cat might be simpler.'

Having rattled us with his search for the rat, the doctor rose to his feet and held his hand out for his fee. 'Let her sleep, don't try to wake her up,' he cautioned.

'We aren't insane.' Harshabardhan was incensed.

'Who dares her wake her up?' Gobra trembled. 'She won't spare us if we wake her up.'

'Yes, let her sleep – don't disturb her,' the doctor advised. 'Let her sleep all night.'

'What about the cat?' I asked. 'Is it supposed to stay in her stomach?'

'Don't they say women can't stomach arguments? But cats are argumentative.' Harshabardhan expressed his viewpoint. 'A living tomcat . . .'

'The poor thing has lost its way inside,' I hazarded a guess. 'It can't find its way out of the labyrinth of the intestine.'

'Let it stay inside. She'll have a catnap,' said the doctor, putting his money away. 'You'll have a purrfect wife.'

'No medicines?' Harshabardhan asked him.

'I'll decide after examining her tomorrow,' answered the doctor. 'How heavy do you think the cat is? Seven or eight kilos . . . hmm . . . that's seven kilos of protein. Might lead to indigestion. She'll need some digestive medicine in case of acidity. Or a strong purgative. We'll cross that bridge when we come to it.'

The doctor prepared to close the patient's mouth with care. But it just wasn't easy. The sleeping lady proved as obstinate as a schoolboy. It needed a lot of effort.

'Why did you do that?' I asked curiously.

'What if a dog gets in, chasing the cat? If a dog joins the cat and the rat, no dogtor on earth can save her. Certainly not a quack like me. She'll be hounded by pain.'

Having administered his preventive to prevent a dog from joining the rat-race, the doctor went home doggedly.

13

Harshabardhan Does Some Arithmetic

'Didn't you say we're going to Ranaghat?' Gobardhan asked his brother. 'When are we leaving? Aren't we going to Mama's today?'

'Of course we are,' Harshabardhan answered. 'Go get some money from your Boudi. We need train-fare, don't we?'

Gobra rushed to Harshabardhan's wife. His brother shouted behind him, 'Tell her to get ready. Let her dress up quickly.'

Returning with a hundred-rupee note, Gobra asked, 'Will this do? Boudi asked me to check.'

'More than enough,' answered Harshabardhan. 'I have some change too, that will take care of the taxi. In fact,' he chuckled, 'this is enough for a quick trip to your Mami's house too.'

'Mami's house? Is that different from Mama's?' Gobra was astonished.

'Ever seen a Mami?'

'Of course I have. With Mama. A pair of Mamas and Mamis. Not once but hundreds of times.'

'Not that Mami, you fool. The kind of Mami who has no Mama. This Mami can't have a Mama.'

'Impossible!' Gobra dismissed the possibility. Mamas are like poets, born to their position. Mamas are born, but Mamis are made. All you have to do to be a Mama is to born as someone's mother's brother, but Mamis have to be ushered in with greater ceremony. Only when a Mama marries is there a Mami. Mamis don't grow on their own like teeth.'

'Not that Mami. An Egyptian Mami. I mean mummy.'

'Who's Egypt? Never heard of him. What kind of Mama is he of ours?'

'Egypt isn't our Mama. I'll show you the Egyptian mummy that's displayed in the museum. After Mama's house, we'll visit mummy's.'

At the museum Harshabardhan's wife was dumbfounded. 'This is your Egyptian mummy? In such a terrible condition?'

'It's dead, after all. Died thousands of years ago. How can you maintain your looks once you're dead? Do you suppose I'll look as I do now when I'm dead?'

'Dead wrong,' said Harshabardhan's wife. 'May you never die.'

'They've used medicines to preserve the mummy,' Harshabardhan elaborated.

'An ancient corpse. Now I get it. Really ancient.'

A label attached to the mummy's coffin said B.C. 2299. Gobra drew his brother's attention to it. 'What's this, Dada? What's this number for?'

Harshabardhan had noticed the label too. Nodding, he said, 'Don't you see? It's the number of the car that ran over the girl.'

'Oh, poor thing. Died under the wheels of a car.' Mrs Harshabardhan was distressed. 'That's why I keep telling you to be careful and watch where you're going. But you never listen. I hope this teaches you a lesson.'

'Heh hehe, no car can run over me.' Harshabardhan laughed away the threat. 'Have you seen my bulk, my dear? Any car that makes the mistake of colliding with me will itself be overturned.' Laughing, Harshabardhan lit a cigarette.

'What if it's a truck?' asked Gobardhan.

'I'm having no truck with trucks.'

A museum official appeared, saying, 'No smoking here.'

'But why? I paid for it, not you,' retorted Harshabardhan. 'You're not my mummy to tell me what to do. Nor can this mummy here dictate to me.'

'Yes this mummy can,' said the official. 'Smoking is forbidden in this room.'

'What if someone smokes?'

'He'll have to pay a fine. Fifty rupees. Can't you see the notice right here?'

He was right. A notice was pasted on the wall. *Smoking is forbidden. Fifty rupees fine.*

'I can't put it out yet. I just lit it. Here's your fine.' Harshabardhan handed over a hundred-rupee note.

'I don't have change,' said the official. 'I can't return fifty rupees?'

'What to do now?' Harshabardhan became anxious on the official's behalf. 'Why don't you have one too, Gobra? The double fine will account for the hundred rupees.'

'Really, Dada!' Gobardhan lowered his eyes. 'How can I smoke in front of you? It's different when I'm alone . . .'

'Then you have a smoke, my dear. Just try one.'

'Oh for heaven's sake,' his wife grimaced.

'Well then. You might as well have one.' Harshabardhan gave the official a cigarette and left with his wife and brother. Outside, they took a taxi to Sealdah Station.

At the station he remembered. 'Oh no, we have no money for the train. I gave away all the money I had at the museum – hundred rupees to meet the mummy's demand. Now where do we get the seventeen rupees seven annas for three tickets to Ranaghat? Have you got any money, Gobra? Or you, my dear?'

'How would I have any?' his wife answered. 'Do you think I keep money in my pocket? Do you think I even have a pocket?' Without replying, Gobra just turned his pockets inside out.

'We're in trouble,' said Harshabardhan, scratching his head. 'You have packets but no pockets, my dear?' He sighed.

'Let's go back home, Dada,' suggested Gobra.

'Are you mad? Go back after coming all this way? All we need to do is get there somehow. We can easily ask Mama for the return fare.'

'As they say, you can make any demand of your Mama,' said Gobra.

'But how do we get there? The money I have,' Harshabardhan rummaged through his pocket, 'is enough for a half-ticket, nothing more. We'll manage.'

'What do you mean?' Harshabardhan's wife objected. 'Three adults travel on a single half-ticket?'

'How is that possible, Dada?' Gobardhan added his opposition to his sister-in-law's.

'Of course it's possible. You just have to be mathematically inclined. Mathematics will get us there.'

Without wasting further words, Harshabardhan bought a third-class half-ticket to Ranaghat. 'Let's get there somehow, then we'll see. We'll return by first class, you'll see.'

The Ranaghat Local was standing at the platform. They got into an empty compartment and sat down.

Harshabardhan said, 'You two sit beneath the seat, not on it. I'll sit on it alone.'

'Why? Are you the lord governor?'

'You're actually asking? Where are your tickets? The ticket-checker will be here any minute. When he sees you're travelling without tickets, he'll put you in jail. Go get in there quickly. You too, Gobra.'

He used the fear of imprisonment to push his brother and wife beneath the seat, sitting down comfortably himself. The train left.

The checker appeared a few stations later. 'Tickets!'

Harshabardhan produced his ticket.

'Half-ticket! What's this!' The checker was astounded. 'A grown up man like you travelling on a half-ticket?'

'Why not?' Harshabardhan protested. 'It's mathematics.'

'Mathematics? What do you mean? I don't understand.'

'You have to have a head for maths to understand. Just look beneath the seat. You'll understand.'

14

Harshabardhan Loses His Temper

Window panes are painful!

Harshabardhan was eternally cheerful, never losing his temper, but even such a man actually lost his temper once.

You remember the song?

Not in Delhi nor in Bombay
Not in Madras nor in Trombay
Neither on a plane or train
While on a steamer ride
The king grew wild

Something similar took place.

After shutting out all sorts of people from his life, Harshbardhan was finally shattered by mere window shutters.

And that single encounter shut out his genial self, making him furious.

Harshabardhan, Gobardhan and I were on a long-distance train. We were on our way to Patna, occupying three berths in a first-class compartment. We had boarded the train at Howrah in the evening, and were due to arrive at Patna the next morning.

Gobra and I were on the two upper berths. Harshabardhan was on one of the lower ones, while the other one was occupied by a gentleman whose destination we didn't know.

Harshabardhan was to go to Patna to open a branch of his furniture business. 'Come with me,' he pleaded. 'You will inaugurate our shop.'

'Why me? All this is for ministers. Aren't there any ministers in Patna?' I was a trifle surprised.

The truth was that I was not the least excited about such things. I always considered inaugurations and unveilings activities for ministers, not for mini stars like me.

'Of course there are,' Harshabardhan answered. 'But I don't particularly get along with these ministers.'

Having administered this statement, he continued, 'And besides, you know what . . .' But Gobardhan interrupted his brother to tell me, 'But you're no less than a minister. You're Dada's chief minister, after all. You're the one who gives him all the bad advice.'

'And another thing,' Harshabardhan completed what he wanted to say, 'All that milk control has meant they don't make sweets in Calcutta anymore. Do you know where all the cooks have gone? They've all gone to Patna to make sweets. If you want some, come along to Patna.'

So I had no choice to but to partner them on the visit to Patna.

The *Bombay Express* clattered along in the darkness, expressing itself noisily.

Suddenly the traveller in the other lower berth pulled down the window pane loudly.

'What's all this?' said Harshabardhan. 'Why did you close the window? Such lovely fresh air.'

'It's cold,' said the man.

'Cold!' Harshabardhan seemed to fall off his lower berth as though it was the upper one. 'Cold? Now? It's barely November. Winter isn't even here yet.' Sitting up, he raised the window pane, taking a deep breath. 'Aaaah! Such a lovely breeze!'

'It's freezing my bones,' the man responded, lowering it again.

'Freezing your bones! Can't you see I'm just wearing a thin kurta?' Harshabardhan raised the pane.

'I can see it's thin. But what about underneath? You've got a thick coat on and warmers too . . .'

'No,' I had to protest. 'That's not a coat, that's his flesh. Can't you see how fat he is? And what you're referring to as a warmer is only his paunch . . .'

'A coat of flesh is no different from a coat. It keeps you warm too. As effective as a coat. Doesn't let the wind freeze your bones. But on my skeletal frame even a warmer is no protection from the cold.' The man did appear to shiver. 'And I've forgotten my scarf too. Do you know I have sensitive tonsils? Even the slightest chill gives me a sore throat.' Down went the pane again.

'Fresh air is very healthy. It never aggravates the tonsils. It can't,' declared Harshabardhan, dignifiedly raising the pane.

'Not yours, perhaps, but it aggravates mine. How can it do anything to you – you've got a thick muffler wrapped around your throat.'

'Muffler round my throat?' Harshabardhan rolled his eyes upwards, as though he wanted me as a witness.

'No, he isn't wearing a muffler,' I had to intervene. 'You say you have weak tonsils, but I can see you have weak eyes too. I don't know the name for that thick object you see around his throat. If he's been a dog you could call it a dog-collar of skin, but we can't be dogmatic about these things,' I added, muffling Harshabardhan's protests. 'In his case we could call it the belly of the neck, or even a flesh necklace, though it actually means more of neck, not less.'

'Why should I need a collar?' Harshabardhan threw a burning glance at me. 'Is anyone trying to collar me?'

'That's just what I'm saying,' I tried to soothe him. 'It would have been a dog-collar if you'd been a dog. But I canine say you're one, can I?'

'At least you've got something covering your tonsils,' said our co-passenger, lowering the window pane once more. 'Anyway, I don't want to get into an argument. All I meant was that I don't want to take risks.'

Harshabardhan raised the pane once again. 'I can't breathe if it's hot. Stale air is bad for health. I cannot abide a polluted atmosphere,' he said, his spherical frame shaking with agitation.

'Do you want to murder me?' The other man lowered the window at once. 'A cold will lead to a cough, a cough to coffee . . . I mean to typhoid, and then to pneumonia . . .'

'And then to a new mania. Death.' Gobardhan added sarcastically from the upper berth.

'Is that what you want? What sort of person are you?' The man lowered the window-pane with a bang.

'And what do you want? That I start hiccuping in this stale, poisoned air, from that to asthma, then tuberculosis, then cancer, then diarrhoea, and finally choke to death. Is that what you want?'

Harshabardhan raised the window.

So they went on, alternately altering the position of the window-pane, their altercation mounting. And thus the train reached Kharagpur.

As soon as the *Bombay Express* came to a stop, Harshabardhan stormed out of the compartment. 'I'm going to the guard to complain about you.'

'I'm going too.' The other man jumped out as well.

I followed them. Only Gobra stayed back in the compartment to look after the luggage.

The guard listened to both their accusations and shook his head gravely. 'This is a difficult situation. Raising the window pane harms your health, and lowering it harms yours? Have I got it right? Yes, very difficult. Let's take a look. Which compartment did you say it was? That first class one, you say? Is the window open now or closed?'

'I lowered the window-pane,' our co-passenger informed the guard.

'As far as I know the window-pane broke some time ago, I don't believe we have replaced the glass yet. You say you lowered the pane? But isn't that someone's nose poking out of the window?'

'My brother Gobardhan's,' said Harshabardhan.

'Then the pane is still broken. How else could he be poking his nose through the window. You'd better get into the train quickly, we'll leave any moment, it's time.'

The guard waved his flag, and the engine whistled. Inside the compartment, Harshabardhan turned his attention to Gobra. 'Why must you poke your nose into everything? Who asked you to lean out of the window?' He began to vent his fury on his brother, losing his temper and slapping Gobra resoundingly.

'Imagine poking your nose out through a glass window. The kind of silly things people do!' I couldn't help chiding Gobra.

15

Harshabardhan Sends for the Doctor

'My wife's very ill. Which doctor do you think I should call?' Harshabardhan asked me.

'Our Dr Ram, of course,' I told him. Then, recalling his high fees, I added, 'Of course, his bill is a bitter pill to swallow, but then his pills always work.'

'My wife's life is at stake. Do you suppose I'm worried about how expensive a doctor might be? This is no time to be pensive about money. All I want is that she should be cured.'

'What's the matter with her?' I asked.

'That is precisely what we cannot tell. One moment she says she has a headache, the next minute it's a toothache, and soon afterwards a stomach ache.'

'This sounds like the kind of illnesses schoolboys have when it's time to go to school.' I said. 'But then who knows a woman's secrets? There's no telling what she might be secreting.'

'Is there something she's expecting, Dada?' Gobra asked. He had accompanied his brother.

'What could she possibly be expecting?' Harshabardhan frowned. 'Do you mean she needs an expectorant? But the problem is not with her throat.'

'I was talking about expecting a child.'

'Is that an illness?' Harshabardhan was enraged by his brother's suggestion. 'That would be a matter of great fortune. Fate has not made us so fortunate.' He sighed.

'Something she ate? No, it's possible Gobra is right,' I said. 'I'm told this is just what happens when you're expecting – headaches, nausea, stomach-cramps . . . who knows, maybe it's the baby who's feeling cramped inside and kicking.'

Which reminded me. A modern sister-in-law of Harshabardhan's had visited him at home once with a bonny baby.

I had taken the little boy in my arms to play with him. The moment I put my finger in his mouth to check whether he had grown any teeth . . . ouch! I jumped in pain.

'What is it?' Harshabardhan's wife grew anxious.

'Nothing,' I replied. 'Just some teeth. This little boy will never lie, he's absolutely toothful.'

'How could you put your finger in his mouth?' Harshabardhan's sister-in-law threw a tantrum. 'Did you ensure you finger is antiseptic?'

'Antiseptic?' I was baffled by this word. 'What on earth does it mean?'

'You call yourself a writer? Don't you have any sense of hygiene?' She held a textbook open under my nose. Noticing that I was paying no attention, she proceeded to read it out herself.

'Before putting any food into a child's mouth it must be meticulously boiled . . .'

'Is a finger food?' Harshabardhan's wife asked.

'Not unless you're talking of finger food,' said Gobra glumly. 'I've seen people suck their own fingers, but never someone else's.'

'It's true that I didn't boil my finger even a little bit,' I stammered out an excuse, 'but your son has bitten it. Here, see for yourself.'

I showed his mother my inflamed finger. With this baby I had obviously bitten off more than I could chew.

'You'd better make arrangements for Dr Ram to visit, then,' I told Harshabardhan. 'Call him at once. Send someone.'

'But will he come?' Harshabardhan looked doubtful.

'What do you mean? Doctors love to make house visits – how's a doctor to make extra money otherwise? Any doctor will visit you at home if you pay the right fee.'

'I did call him, and he had come too. As you know, I rear poultry behind the house – hens and ducks. But those ducks are so ill-mannered that they even come round to the front of the house sometimes. And they made such a noise that day on seeing Dr Ram that . . .'

'Did they need a doctor too?'

'Who knows! What would they need a doctor for? Do they understand medicine? I doubt it. Maybe his enormous bag frightened them, but the doctor got so angry he turned round and went right back, without evening coming into the house.'

'Really?' I was astonished.

'Oh yes. I've sent for him many times since then – with the lure of fat fees. But he's not willing to step anywhere near this house.'

'How strange. But he's the only good doctor hereabouts. There's no one like Dr Ram . . .'

'Can you plead with him to come?' Harshabardhan entreated me.

'Let me try,' I said, and set off.

Doctors really could be obstinate. Take Dr Ram himself.

When Bini fell down and cut herself, I went to the doctor's chamber to ask him to come home. But as soon as I said, 'A cut from a fall . . .'

'A cut? Did it bleed?'

'It did bleed a little, yes.'

'That's alarming! A fall and bleeding here in Calcutta is very dangerous, let me check for myself . . .'

Taking the thermometer out of his medical bag, he thrust it into my mouth.

'Now lie down, quickly.' Without giving me a chance to protest, he forced me down on his examination table.

'Lie down at once. Not another word.'

With the thermometer filling up my mouth how was I to talk anyway? I got no chance to explain. And he took the opportunity to give me an injection with an enormous syringe.

'There. Nothing to worry about anymore. That's the anti-tetanus injection taken care of. No need to fear hydrophobia now.' Taking the thermometer out of my mouth, he checked it and said, 'Excellent. No fever. You're safe.'

With my mouth finally free I managed to tell him, 'There's nothing wrong with me, doctor. I didn't fall or cut myself. It happened to my sister Bini. You didn't even . . .'

'Oh, really? Why didn't you tell me earlier? Still, what's done is done. I'd better go and give her an injection too. Did you put some Dettol on the cut? Or some iodine?'

'Yes I did.'

'Then it should be all right. Still, let's go and give her the injection. You can never be too careful.'

Very considerately he did not charge for Bini's injection, though I had to pay for mine. Plus his fee for a home visit.

This was the stubborn Dr Ram I would have to visit. I was quite apprehensive, to tell the truth.

I would have to bring the subject up diplomatically.

Entering his chamber, I greeted him from a safe distance.

'Doctor. I'm here to request you for a home visit. But not for myself. I'm not ill, nothing's wrong with me. I haven't fallen down or cut myself. Don't go and give me an injection like last time.'

Finally I mentioned Harshabardhan. At which he charged towards me, if not to give me an injection, definitely to hand me a rejection.

'No, I'll never visit his house. Not while I'm alive, not in this lifetime. They're very rude . . .'

'Harshabardhan-babu and rudeness! Please don't say that. Not even his enemies can make this claim.'

'What else but rude? Are you telling me it's polite to invite someone home and then insult him?'

'He invited you home and insulted you? I don't believe it. You must have misunderstood. You're so s . . .' About to blurt out the word stubborn, I controlled myself.

'Even if he personally didn't insult me, he used his ducks for the purpose. Which is the same thing.'

'Insulted you though his ducks. I don't believe you.'

'You think I'm lying? When his wicked ducks saw me they tore into me in a way I cannot bring myself to repeat.'

'The ducks tore into you? But it's we who tear into ducks. I cannot tell you what a delicious duck roast my sister Putul makes. I can't wait to tear into it the next time she cooks it.'

'Whatever you may say, Harshabardhan-babu's ducks are far from delectable. Quite poisonous, in fact. As soon as they saw me they went quack, quack, vilifying me.' He turned red with rage. 'Am I a quack? Don't I have a medical degree? Just because people say so?'

'Is that it?' I reassured him. 'No, the ducks didn't reveal any secret of yours, they didn't treat you like a sitting duck. They're

English ducks, you see, so they speak in English. What they said didn't exactly mean quack the way you thought of it, it was just their cry. If they'd been Bengali ducks . . . if you translated their words into Bengali, it would merely refer to the cry of ducks.'

'Are you sure? All right then, let's go.'

He agreed to come along. 'Just a minute, let me arrange my bag – this bag is the cause of all my troubles. I have to beg it to behave.'

'If you'd stop your bagriculture . . .' I began, but he interrupted me with a shout. 'Don't be bagressive!'

'No, that's not what I meant. What I meant was . . .'

'What did you mean?'

'I only meant, you know the bagground, the patient is very ill, you need to bagin the treatment at once.'

'But I have to bag this bag of mine. It has everything I need – my thermometer, stethoscope, blood pressure meter, medicines, everything.'

Putting everything in order, the doctor accompanied me with his bag.

But barely had he taken a few steps when he came to an abrupt halt. Stopping in the middle of the road, he started upbraiding me. 'No, I shan't go. I've promised myself not to visit that house so long as the ducks are there, whether they're quacking in English or in Bengali. I cannot break my promise. Forgive me.'

He took a stand and then didn't stand there anymore, winding his way back home.

Really, how silly Dr Ram could be sometimes.

What could I do? I explained everything to Harshabardhan. 'If you want to save your wife's life get rid of the ducks.' Harshabardhan thought it over sullenly. Then he said, sighing, 'Oh well, who is your son and who, your wife? Whom do you belong to and who belongs to you? Are the ducks mine?

Do I belong to the ducks? Will the ducks go with me when I die? No one is born with ducks, though they spend their life ducking blows. What joy will the ducks bring me? Whose ducks am I looking after?' He sang a swan song for his pets. 'Money is meaningless. Let the ducks go. They were expensive. Lots of money wasted, that's all.'

He pondered over something, holding his head in his hand, and then moaned, 'No, I cannot send my wife to the hospital. I have to be inhospitable to the ducks.'

Unlocking the poultry door, he drove the ducks out. They danced away amidst the collective joy of the neighbourhood urchins.

When I told the doctor about the departure of the ducks, he left for Harshabardhan's house, bag in hand.

As soon as he arrived Harshabardhan handed him two crisp hundred rupee notes as his fee and took him to his wife's room. We followed.

'What seems to be the problem?' the doctor asked the patient.

'My head aches, my teeth hurt, I'm cold, and I have stomach cramps.'

'Indeed!' The doctor reflected on this gravely before drawing Harshabardhan outside the room.

'Seems to be a very difficult case,' he said, looking grim.

'Will my wife survive?'

'No, there's nothing to worry about. I'm not apprehending anything extreme. However, nine out of ten patients die from such illnesses. Only one survives.'

'In that case . . .' Harshabardhan's terror grew tenfold.

'What! Then there's no hope for Boudi,' said Gobra tearfully and began to sob.

'She'll live,' the doctor reassured us. 'Nine of my patients suffering from this illness have died already. She's the tenth. No one can kill her. Anyway, let me examine the patient carefully now. Wait in the other room. Don't you enter this one.' He drove us away.

The three of us sat down in the next room. Harshabardhan was pale with fear. And Gobra's face had shrunk to resemble a dried coconut shell.

'Headache, toothache, stomachache – of course it's serious,' I said. To lighten the mood I threw some light on the illness. 'One ache is bad enough, but three!'

'The illness is spreading through her veins, Dada,' commented Gobra. 'Didn't she say all her efforts to feel better have been in vain?'

'This illness is definitely venomous,' I said, showing off my medical knowledge. 'It will need an antidote.'

Dr Ram appeared at the door. 'Can you get me a rasp? Or at least a chisel?'

Harshabardhan brought both.

'What's he going to do with a rasp, Dada?' Gobra asked. 'Is he making raspberry juice as medicine?'

'Maybe,' I agreed. 'His voice did sound rasping when he asked.'

Harshabardhan clutched his head with his hands in silence.

'He might need the rasp for the teeth too,' I continued. 'Dental caries also causes toothache. Maybe he'll file it off with the rasp. We're fallible when it comes to teeth. Only when our teeth fall off do we realize their value. Bad teeth can cause many diseases – colic, chest pain, indigestion, even arthritis.'

Dr Ram peeped in at the door again. 'Do you have a hammer?'

Harshabardhan brought him a hammer.

'What does he want a hammer for, Dada?' Gobra jumped. 'Is he going to bang at her teeth to cure her toothache?'

'No idea,' sighed Harshabardhan. 'People do say he goes at illnesses with hammer and tongs.'

'We can see why,' responded Gobra.

'Maybe he will hammer on her head, not her teeth,' I said. 'Isn't there something called shock treatment?'

'That's the wrong skull of thought,' said Gobra. 'But now it will be hammered home to Dada. He'll never see Boudi's sweet smile again. To think destiny held a toothless sister-in-law for me!' Gobra lamented his fate.

'I've heard that hammering on the head cures headaches,' I said, trying to offer hope.

'No head, no headache,' responded Harshabardhan.

'Shock treatment means giving a sudden shock to cure an illness,' I told him. 'I believe difficult diseases can be cured this way. Dr Ram is trying his best.'

'Then there's nothing more to be said.' Harshabardhan gave up.

'Let the doctor do what he can, don't come in his way,' I added a postscript.

'Can you give me a saw? A small one all do.' The doctor appeared the door again. There was no lack of saws in Harshabardhan's furniture factory. Bringing one for the doctor, he said despondently, 'Who knows what will happen now.'

'I think he's planning to saw Boudi open and bring the child out,' Gobardhan explained. 'Boudi will be cut into two and the baby will die. This will really cut you up, Dada.'

'Your wife will survive,' I reassured him. 'Haven't you seen how famous magicians can saw a woman into two pieces and then put her together again? Our P.C. Sorcar does it all the time. Well-known doctors can do magic too.'

But Harshabardhan could stay still no longer. He jumped to his feet. 'Does he think he can saw my wife in two in front of my eyes without my doing anything about it?' He stormed into the next room, followed by Gobardhan. I trailed behind them.

'What do you think you're doing?' he snarled at the doctor. 'Are you planning to hack my wife into two pieces? Why? Why? My friend the writer here may be a hack, but my wife isn't one. Why does she need this sort of . . .'

'Your wife? What are you talking about?' Dr Ram interrupted him. 'I'm busy with my bag. I haven't even examined your wife yet. This blasted bag goes turns very stubborn sometimes. I've tried everything – the hammer, the chisel, the rasp, but nothing's worked. I just can't open it. I'm going to saw it open now. All my instruments and medicines, even my thermometer, are in there. I have to get them out before I can treat your wife. I can cure all the illnesses in the world but I can't cure my bag. This bag makes me absolutely sick.'

16

How to Rob a Thief

'Alas! Imagine dying helplessly at the hands of thieves,' lamented Harshabardhan.

'We may be helpless, Dada, but we're not dead yet.' Gobra corrected his brother's error.

'But we might be killed any moment, considering the rogues whose hands we've fallen into. I can't even tell how far from Calcutta they've brought us.'

'Who knows where we are.'

'Can't even go out for a walk and try to find out.'

'Even if you could, how would you know, Dada? It's not like the name of the place is engraved on the earth.'

'On people's tongues.'

Gobra's wonder knew no bounds. 'Is the name of a place written on people's tongues?'

'Don't talk like an idiot. Can't you tell from their language? Whether they're speaking Bangla or Assamese or Hindi or Oriya will tell us where we've been brought. Purnea or Cuttack, Chhapra or Ara, Guwahati or Goa, Bombay or Madras . . . or some other stranger place.'

'I can bet it isn't Bombay,' said Gobra. 'Bombay is about a thousand miles from Calcutta. They've brought us only a hundred miles or so. And suppose we're in Madras . . . even so . . .'

'Even so?'

'Even so you won't be able to tell. The people in Madras all speak Tamil. How will you identify the language? And besides,' Gobra unravelled the problem further, 'if we're taken there, we'll die of starvation.'

'Why should we die? Don't they have shops? We can buy food, can't we?'

'Even if you want to eat, how will they know what to give you? How will they even understand what you want to eat? The people of Madras won't understand your mad rush for food, since you don't speak their language. They cannot gauge your needs.'

Someone came down the stairs from the terrace, humming. Not a rough-looking ruffian or one of the kidnappers. A complete stranger.

'And who might you be? Where did you turn up from, humming?' The astonished Harshabardhan managed to find words.

'Of course, hummingbirds can also hum and turn up from nowhere,' Gobra added. 'But for a human being to drop humming from the skies is not a humdrum matter.'

'And how is it that you appeared from the terrace?' asked Harshabardhan. 'People normally enter downstairs and climb up. From the front door to the roof . . .'

'Surely you don't live on the roof. We've never seen you up there. And when did you manage to climb up? We didn't notice. We went up to the terrace ourselves once, we never saw you there,' said Gobra.

'How would you see me when I wasn't even there? I don't belong hereabouts,' the man informed them. 'I'm here to help you escape.'

'What! Help us escape! But these people have stolen us. We've been abducted.'

'I will abduct the abducted. That's why I'm here.'

'I see. You belong to a different gang.'

'No, we're not thieves. Don't insult us by calling us thieves,' he protested vehemently.

'Burglars, then?'

The man gurgled with laughter. 'Burglars! We don't even consider thieves and burglars members of the human race. Is that even a profession? Are stealing and cheating worthy of gentlemen? Don't accuse us of all this.'

'Then who are you?'

'We're far superior to thieves.'

'I don't understand.'

'You will. All in good time. There's no time now, we'll explain afterwards. Just tell me whether you want to escape or not. Are you willing to be saved from these rogues?'

'Of course!' The brothers sounded excited. 'But how? The front door is locked, and there are guards keeping an eye on us . . .'

'Not that way. I will help you escape via the roof. Using the route I took into the house.' He started climbing the stairs to the terrace. 'Come with me.'

Following him to the roof, Harshabardhan discovered a tree directly behind the house, growing against its wall, full of leaves. Just right for Harshabardhan and Gobardhan to escape.

'See the tree?' The upwardly mobile man pointed it out to them. 'See how it has practically flung itself on the roof? That's the route I took. You can climb on its branches, can't you?'

'Of course we can. Trees are our business. We're timber merchants, and we're always opening branches,' Harshabardhan told him. 'We've felled so many trees, then felt the joy of turning them into furniture. And as for Gobra, he's been brought up by trees. He used to live on a mango tree most of the time, like a monkey.'

'Only when the mangoes had ripened,' Gobra protested. 'Not all the time. And never round the year.'

Using the branches to climb up and then down the tree to the ground, Harshabardhan heaved a sigh of relief. 'Thank goodness. Free of the thieves at last.'

'We may be free of the thieves,' Gobra whispered, 'but who knows whose clutches we have fallen into instead.'

Following them down the tree, the stranger came up to them. 'Come with me, my car is waiting. Just up the road.'

In the car Harshabardhan asked, 'Where are we going now?'

'You'll see in a few minutes.'

In fifteen minutes or so they had reached a large city. 'Which city is this?' Gobra enquired.

'Calcutta.'

'Are you joking?' The brothers smiled in disbelief. 'We were a hundred miles from Calcutta. And you claim we're in Calcutta after such a short journey? Impossible!'

'Belgachhia a hundred miles from Calcutta? I had no idea!' Their companion was no less astonished.

'You think we don't know Belgachhia? If we were in Belgachhia, where was the hospital? And the bridge?'

'We didn't take the road through Belgachhia. We drove through Dhakuria to avoid the rogues.'

'If this is Calcutta why doesn't it look familiar? Has it changed so much in just a few days?'

'That's Calcutta for you. Changes every day. Every hour, every minute. It isn't easy to recognize Calcutta.'

Soon they were at Rashbehari Avenue. 'Oh yes, this is Calcutta all right!' Harshabardhan was elated. 'There's a tram.

Trams are the surest sign of being in Calcutta, you know, Gobra. There are rickshaws and cars and carts everywhere – even in the villages – but you won't see a tram anywhere except in Calcutta.'

Veering off the road with tram tracks, the car drove though several streets and roads and finally entered a residential neighbourhood through a narrow lane.

'Doesn't this area look familiar, Dada?' Gobra said. 'Looks like our locality. Just like the area we live in, don't you think?'

'How could that be possible?' Harshabardhan said, running a keen eye over their surroundings. 'But then the fact is that most neighbourhoods in Calcutta are similar. All the houses have front doors. Slums next door. Boys playing with rubber balls on the streets, or battering things claiming that it's cricket.'

'Battering?' Gobra wondered what that meant. 'What sort of ring is that?'

'Battering? That's when they err with the bat.'

'Oh, you mean that game with a bat and a ball. I was wondering how a ring came into it.'

'Why is this road so bumpy?' Harshabardhan asked the man.

'They're laying telephone lines or water pipes or something beneath the road, so they've dug it up. The car won't go any further. We'd better get off.'

'You really think it's like our neighbourhood? There was so much space in our area, children would play football in the abandoned plots of land, but here? Only high-rise buildings everywhere, check for yourself.'

Their companion took them into an empty house. 'This is our home for now,' he told them. There were no shutters on the windows, which were wide open. The house was deserted. The rooms were grimy, full of rubbish. Harshbardhan wrinkled his nose at the sight and the smells. 'There's nothing here, not even a table. Looks more like a stable to me.'

'You're right, Dada,' exclaimed Gobra. 'But then why should you have problems in a stable? Half your name is Harsha, and where do horses live but in stables?'

Harshabardhan was furious at his brother's attempt at humour. Without answering, he told the man, 'Then you'd better look for a cowshed for my other half.'

'Cowshed?'

'I'll be fine in a stable, but my brother can't survive in one. He needs one.'

'You're asking me to find a cowshed for your brother?'

'His name is Gobardhan. As you know, it refers to cowdung. Which is usually to be found in cowsheds, where it just lies scattered about.'

But the man wasn't interested in such jokes. 'I see. Well, call it a stable or a cowshed, this is where we'll spirit you away for now.'

'Spirit us away?' The brothers appeared most dispirited.

'Are we going to be murdered?' Gobra wanted to know.

'Why should we murder you? We don't murder people. Didn't I tell you we aren't thieves or burglars?'

'But you didn't tell us what you are.'

'I said we're far superior to thieves. We rob from them. They only steal, but we're made of steel.'

'Now I understand,' said Harshabardhan. And though he felt as if a weight had been lifted from his shoulders, he knew there was a long wait ahead.

'Is this your robbers' colony then?'

'Neither a robbers' colony nor a robber plantation . . .' The man was about to reveal the name of the area with great fanfare when Gobra's scream interrupted them. 'Look!'

Pointing at a wall, he shouted, 'This is definitely our neighbourhood, Dada. This is our house, in fact. Don't you see your name written there . . .'

Harshabardhan looked. His name was indeed written on the wall. Sri Sri Harshabardhan. And, below it, Sri Gobardhan.

'It IS our house. But who has done this to our house?' Harshabardhan practically sobbed. 'Our furniture, our beds, cupboards, sofas, tables, chairs . . . where are they?'

'Where are the fridge, the fans, the lights, the windows . . .' complained Gobra.

'All stolen,' clarified the robber. 'Do you suppose thieves leave anything behind in a house in Calcutta if no one's living in it, if the owner is absent? It's hard enough keeping thieves at bay when you're home, and you two have been away for quite some time.'

'But such outrageous theft right here in Calcutta?'

'Consider yourself lucky you've found the house intact. So far they've just taken your furniture and doors and windows, if you'd come back a little later you'd have found the bricks and wood and rafters all taken away in trucks – right under the neighbours' noses. All you'd have found is an empty plot of land. And if you came back even later, you'd have discovered that someone else had grabbed your land too and built a seven-storied building on it. You wouldn't even have recognized the house. There would have been no sign of your original home.'

'Boudi's at her parents'. Who was going to look after the house?' Gobra rued their fortune. 'There was no one to look after us either. When the kidnappers found us orphaned they just took us away.'

'There you have it. With the housewife missing, the house is so dirty. Who's going to clean? Who will dust and wipe? Now you have to make a clean break from the past and do it yourself.'

'To hell with the house, who will wipe our tears away?' Gobardhan poured salt on his brother's wound.

'Why should tears have to be wiped? Do you think I'm weeping for your sister-in-law? You can weep if you want to. Weep and sweep.'

'That's all very well but I haven't solved this mystery,' said the robber, pointing to the wall. 'It says Sri Sri Harshabardhan there. What does that mean?'

'It means it's him,' explained Gobra. 'He's standing right in front of you. He's Harshabardhan, and I . . . I am . . .'

'No need to say anymore,' said the robber. 'You needn't talk about yourself. You're the second one. Isn't that so? I was told you are important people, but I didn't know how important.'

'What's so important about us?' asked Gobardhan testily.

'The Sri Sri. I find it hideous. Why Sri Sri with the name of ordinary people? That's usually kept for holy men. Sri Sri Krishna, Sri Sri Ramkrishna . . .'

'Do you mean he isn't a holy man? Have you seen him? If he isn't whole, who is?'

'Everyone's whole. Wholly themselves.'

'And moreover, my wife will also have a wholesome brother-in-law in him,' added Gobra.

'No, I'm no one's brother-in-law yet. This fellow isn't even married. But yes, my wife is visiting her parents to find a bride for him. In case any of her cousins can help . . . let's see.' Harshabardhan revealed the truth.

'That would be very helpful,' the robber agreed. 'Considering the state of the house, it will need two housewives to clean everything up. Even a pair may not be enough.'

'No one can match my Boudi,' declared Gobra. 'She's incomparable. She's divine. Now you know why her husband uses a Sri Sri before his name. He has divined that she is a goddess.'

'And even if I'm not divine myself, I'm no vine either,' Harshabardhan pointed out. 'Not exactly slender, am I?'

'Then yours is a wholly holy family,' said the robber. 'Now, if you don't want to be holed up here, just write a couple of cheques quickly, will you? We'll check out from your house at once.'

No sooner had he said this than a commotion arose outside the house.

'Dacoits?' The robber peeped out and discovered a horse-drawn carriage standing outside the house, piled high with things. A formidable woman had got off the carriage and was directing the coachman to unload everything. Everything was piled up on the doorstep.

She was now engaged in a furious argument over the fairness of the fare. Their voices rose successively, and the coachman's prospects did not appear rosy. The neighbourhood reverberated with their screams.

'My goodness, it really is a dacoit,' exclaimed the robber. 'Robbers can be rubbed out by dacoits. I'm off.' He escaped through the back door.

'What kind of dacoit?' said Gobra, peeping apprehensively through the window. The next moment he jumped with joy. 'It's Boudi! She's back. We've been saved, nothing more to be afraid of.'

'Except of your sister-in-law,' said Harshabardhan glumly. 'We'll have to live in fear of her again, that's all.'

17

Gobardhan's Windfall

Harshabardhan had to go to Howrah Station on an errand with his brother in tow. That was where he saw the notice. He hadn't noticed it earlier.

'Have you read that?' He pointed out the notice board to Gobra. 'You should.'

'It's just an advertisement,' grimaced Gobardhan. 'What's in there to read?'

'Plenty. They don't teach anything in schools. Do you learn how the world functions? You don't. But you can learn everything there is to learn just by reading advertisements.'

'You can read them, Dada, you can learn. That's enough for both of us.' Gobardhan expressed his adversity to advertisements.

'I learnt a lesson yesterday even without reading it,' snorted Harshabardhan. 'It would have helped to have read it earlier. Now I can only regret that I didn't.'

Gobra found this mysterious. 'What happened yesterday?'

'You remember our family priest leaving for home yesterday? I went to Sealdah Station to buy a ticket for him. If only I'd noticed the advertisement then . . .'

'You astonish me, Dada. You want to read a notice put up at Howrah Station all the way from Sealdah Station? However farsighted you may be, how is that possible?' Gobra couldn't keep himself from pointing out that his brother was confusing history with geography.

'That's how shortsighted I am,' said Harshabardhan, explaining the previous day's events in detail.

There was a long queue in front of the booking office at Sealdah too – just as long as the one here. Just as he joined the crowd, someone came up to him unbidden and said, a portly person like you will find it hard to manage. Give me the money, I'll buy the ticket for you. I have to get one for myself too, so I have to join the queue anyway.

Harshabardhan gave him the money for the ticket, and then kept a strict watch on him.

The man advanced slowly. The tail of the queue was a long way back. The man was moving forward along the tail. Harshabardhan was scanning both the head and the tail with an eagle eye, but in an instant the man had vanished somewhere. Vaporized.

Finishing his story, Harshabardhan returned his attention to the notice, where it said in bold, bright letters, 'Beware! Thieves and pickpockets nearby!'

Transferring his suspicious gaze to his brother, he said, 'Do you understand now?'

'I do. But why are you looking at me so suspiciously?' Gobra snarled. 'I may be nearby, but I'm not a thief or pickpocket – let me tell you that clearly.'

'Did I say that? Thieves need to be clever – you're not intelligent enough to be one. And that's what I'm afraid of. There are so many criminals all over this city,' elaborated Harshabardhan. 'On the streets, in post-offices, in railway stations, everywhere. Full of scoundrels. Go to the post-office and someone will offer to get your money-order made for you.

As for the railway station, the less said the better – most of the people who seem to be hovering around to buy tickets are only interested in making off with other people's money. Frauds, all of them. There are two cheats inside each of them. I can now recognize them a mile away – all these nasty types skulking around to nab innocent victims. Beware from now on.'

Harshabardhan assumed a rather harsh expression.

'Don't worry, Dada,' Gobardhan tried to reassure him. 'No one can take me for a ride. I'm not an easy customer.'

'That's just the point – you won't ride away anywhere. And they can cheat not just you but every one of your forefathers. They're making fools out of people far cleverer than you, all the time. That's how they make a living.'

Harshabardhan offered various examples of their cheating ways. How they pass off gleaming brass as gold, supposedly picking up these so-called golden items on the street and selling them; how they display one ten-rupee note as two; how they play tricks with three cards on the pavement – he described the thrilling exploits of these charlatans, nearly exploding in rage.

'Ma did tell me not to go to Calcutta,' said Gobra. 'They kidnap people in Calcutta and pass them off to the tea estates in Assam. Like counterfeit money.'

'Yes, your mother knows everything,' Harshabardhan sneered at his brother. 'That was long ago. They won over innocent people with cups of tea and then packed them off to the tea-estates. After which it was a case of lifelong labour. But all this happened in the past. These people are much worse. They will gobble you up and empty you out without killing you. They'll drain you of everything you have. They will extract all your possessions while distracting you. You won't even get to know. By the time you do, it'll be useless.'

Gobardhan could not provide satisfactory answers to any of the questions represented in his brother's expression.

After Harshabardhan's warning, the days passed in great fear. When he went out he walked warily, watching his step all the way, for fear of treading on a modern-day cheat. He looked behind him all the time, to ensure no one was following him. He didn't dare talk to anyone, not even having the courage to whisper to the stone statues he met in parks.

Every day he had to recount the details of his safe perambulations to his brother. The exciting account of how he had avoided anything suspicious, not just cheats and frauds but even policemen. Leave alone bumping into a charlatan, he had not allowed anyone to bump him off.

But Gobra got into big trouble one day. He lost his way and found himself in an unfamiliar part of town. He didn't dare stop anyone and ask for directions. He was doomed if anyone got to know that he was lost. His mother had warned him about the tea gardens, and his brother, to be on guard. Both warnings were equally horrifying. Gobardhan would have to gird his loins against both of them.

He wandered about all afternoon without finding his way back. But he felt a sudden stab of doubt. Someone was following him.

Looking over his shoulder, he discovered he was right. The man had been hovering around for quite some time, as though he had something to say.

That was it. Gobra panicked. The more he tried to give his follower the slip, turning this way and that to confuse him, the easier it seemed for the man to keep him in sight. Utter disaster!

Gobardhan turned abruptly into a sweet shop, putting down a rupee and taking a box of jalebis to a table to munch on them. Would you believe it! His pursuer followed him in a little later, buying himself some samosas and kachoris and sitting down at a table.

Beware, thieves and pickpockets are nearby! The notice and his brother's warning were both being proved right. The man would pick his pocket at the first opportunity. His wallet would soon be lighter and his heart, heavier.

The middle-aged man seemed a very strange character indeed. Sitting opposite Gobardhan, he sipped his tea and stared with astonished eyes, as though he had never seen anything so extraordinary. Feeling extremely uncomfortable, Gobra began to squirm.

'You look very familiar,' the man began a conversation. 'Have I seen you somewhere before?'

'Hmm,' said Gobra, shooting out of his chair and racing away, muttering to himself, 'You claim to have seen me before. But I have never seen your blasted face anywhere. Still I know who you are – you're a . . . a . . . however you may be, there's no need to get to know you, I say no to knowing you. Goodbye.'

He tried to get away from the man, but, strangely, the man refused to let the distance grow between them. He stuck to Gobra like a shadow.

At his wits' end, Gobra circled a park thrice before entering and sitting down on a bench. The man chased him into the park and sat down – on the same bench.

He had tried hard to lose himself in the crowd, but he hadn't succeeded in evading his eye. Instead of trying any more, Gobra sat stiffly on the bench in apprehension. What now?

The man began talking in an intimate tone. 'I recognized you perfectly, young master. You're a member of the Mitra family, everyone in Calcutta knows you. I recognized you at first glance.'

Oh my god. He was calling Gobardhan a *mitra* – a friend. Gobardhan was stunned. The man was obviously an enemy.

'You're the late Digambar Mitra's son. I recognized you.'

Gobra was silent. Although this seemed less hostile, he wasn't going to play host to this man.

'I was wondering why you looked familiar. Finally I've got it. I saw you the other day at your office – it wasn't all that long ago.'

Gobardhan could barely stammer out a denial.

But the man stamped out his stammer and continued, 'Have you considered my proposal? I wanted to buy your house in Beltala, and you said you'd think it over. I hope you have no objection.'

Gobra wanted to say, 'You can dig as deep as you like into this Digambar Mitra's family but you won't find me.' He also wanted to add that the reference to a house in Beltala rang no bells in his mind. But he didn't get the chance.

For the man just went on talking. 'No, I won't take no for an answer. I want to settle it here and now. Here's five hundred rupees, consider this my advance. No, you mustn't wave me away. My wife loves the house, you know. No more objections, please. Very well, let's say a thousand rupees as advance – I'll pay the rest once the price is settled. This is all I have right now – please accept this and let's seal a deal.'

Refusing to entertain any protests, the man forced a wad of notes into Gobardhan's hands and ran out of the park lest Digambar's offspring change his mind.

Gobra sat with his mouth open.

Leaving the park absent-mindedly a little later, he managed to find his way back home.

Harshabardhan was waiting for him impatiently. Had his brother lost his way? Or had he been kidnapped? He was about to write Gobra off his books when his sibling appeared.

'And where were you?'

'Doing a little business, Dada.'

'Business? Didn't I warn you not to fall into the clutches of a cheat? All these shrewd people extract money from naive young men like you under the pretext of a business deal. They show off their prowess on the stock market to sell the company. Didn't I tell you over and over? But you chose to fall into their hands. How much did they cheat you out of? How much have you lost?'

'I haven't lost any money, in fact I've made some. I haven't exactly been cheated. But can I tell you something, Dada? It's more difficult not to cheat someone than to be cheated – that's what I've realized. I just sold my house in Beltala . . . I haven't exactly sold it yet, only taken an advance, not a large sum, about a thousand. Here.'

He let the currency notes fly about in the breeze of the ceiling fan.

'What! My brother, the late Poundrabardhan's son, a scion of the Bardhan dynasty – a cheat? Someone who defrauds others?'

The currency notes swirled in the air and Harshabardhan's eyes whirled as he followed them.

He had never imagined there would be a cheat in his family. This unimaginable possibility made him gulp.

'I cannot say whether I cheated him, but I did try not to. I tried my best, Dada. I told him I do not belong to Digambar Mitra's family. But he just wouldn't listen. What was I to do?'

18

Harshabardhan Posts a Letter

Harshabardhan's wife came up to him to take his coat when he returned from office.

Then, fixing her baleful eyes, not on Harshabardhan but on the pocket of his coat, she cried, 'Oh no! You forgot to post the letter again! How forgetful you are. How will you ever run a household if you're going to be so absent-minded.'

Thinking of the presence of his body, Harshabardhan was about to say, 'I don't run the household, you do.' But it was doubtful whether this prose poem would reverse her viewpoint. So he simplified what he was about to say. 'That's how it is, my dear. I am absent and you mind the household.'

'Enough. Please don't forget to put in the mail tomorrow. Very important letter . . . to my mother . . . and you . . . I reminded you so many times when you were going to work. How do you run your business if something as simple as posting a letter slips your mind?'

'Who said it slipped my mind?' Harshabardhan protested. 'It's definitely there still, mind you.'

'Nonsense. I'll make sure you don't forget tomorrow.'

'Are you planning to tie a knot in my dhoti like last time?' Harshabardhan asked in terror. 'No, I'm not going to office all knotted up.'

He was reminded of people's sniggers last time. Our children are naughty, they said, but your dhoti is knotty. It's knot my doing, he had said to get away on that occasion.

'Not a knot again?'

'No, not this time.'

'Thank goodness.' He was relieved that there would be no more entanglements. His frown softened.

'No knots. But I'll ensure you don't forget to post the letter tomorrow.'

'It would have been fine if you'd written the letter to me instead of your mother,' said Harshabardhan, making a clean breast of things. 'It could just have stayed in my breast pocket.'

He remembered the days soon after their wedding. His wife would write to him from her parents' house, letters that he would carry with him all the time. He wouldn't part with them for love or for money. Later, of course, the letters only wanted him to part with money. Send more money. The letters would be washed clean when the clothes were sent to the laundry. All the meaning in them would be clear at one go.'

When helping Harshabardhan on with his coat as he was about to leave for office the next morning, his wife reminded him again. 'You won't forget to post the letter, will you?'

'Certainly not! I dare not forget again.'

Must post the letter, must post the letter . . . Harshabardhan went out, muttering the incantation to himself. At the end of the road a young man told him, 'You haven't forgotten the letter, have you?'

'What letter?'

'Your wife's letter. Just reminding you to post it.'

'Really? Did she whisper instructions in your ears?' He strode off angrily. 'Now she has a supporter.'

Barely had he taken a few steps when someone hailed him. 'Just a minute.'

'Me?'

'Yes, you. Have you taken care of the letter yet?'

'What letter? Some official work?'

'No, not official. I was referring to your wife's letter. Have you posted it?'

'That's my responsibility. What business is it of yours?' An enraged Harshabardhan didn't let the conversation continue.

Strange! Word had spread all over already. From his wife, via all the housewives of the neighbourhood, and then to their husbands and brothers-in-law, there was no one who didn't know. He was dying to get out of the locality.

But it wasn't as though he was safe outside.

As he waited for the tram on the main road, a group of schoolboys passed him, chanting, 'Post the letter, don't forget to post the letter.'

He really was astonished now. But where was the time to think of all this? Office time.

Harshabardhan got on the tram as soon as it stopped. But no sooner had he found a seat when the man behind him tapped him on the shoulder.

'If you don't mind . . .'

He looked back in surprise. It wasn't anyone he knew.

'May I tell you something if you don't mind? Have you posted the letter?'

No more surprise. This time he was positively annoyed. What was all this? Why was everyone singing the same tune?

'Why do you ask? Whether I post my letter or not is none of your business.'

'No, it isn't, but I'm telling you because I felt I should. The rest is up to you.'

'How did you know about the letter? Who told you? Was it one of my neighbours?'

'No no no . . .'

'Well then? I don't recall you being related to me or my wife.'

'If it comes to that, it's the theory of relativity.' An amiable smile suffused his face.

Relativity? Harshabardhan stopped to think this over. Instead of the laws of relativity, was the man referring to the in-laws of relativity? And was he a brother-in-law of Harshabardhan's – someone he had paid no attention to since he had eyes only for his sisters-in-law?

'. . . I'm telling you this on your wife's request. It really is no concern of mine.'

'What! My wife asked you to remind me? I don't believe you.'

But still he was left in doubt. How could the man have known unless his wife had told him? It really was too much – why did she have to wash dirty linen in public?

But how had she managed to inform so many people in such a short time? He had a niggling doubt over the whole thing.

Still, no matter how in-lawful this brother was, Harshabardhan had no time to argue with him, for the tram had arrived at his office. He had to get off.

Seated at his desk, he shouted for a glass of water. 'Bearer!'

The bearer ran up to him, stretching his hand out, and said, 'Give it to me.'

'What? Give you what?'

'You're giving me the letter, aren't you?'

'What letter?' Harshabardhan was taken aback. There were stories about someone who had been dying of thirst and had asked for a glass of water, only to be handed half a fruit, but this seemed rather a fruitless question.

'You sent for me to post madam's letter, didn't you?' said the bearer. 'Give me the letter.'

'Who told you that? Get out, you impudent fellow. Imprudent too.' He roared. 'You imbecile.'

But his anger was matched by his surprise. The whole thing appeared extremely strange to him – an impenetrable mystery. He forgot all about this parched throat.

On his way back home in the tram, various people sought him out to ask about the letter. One of them actually said, 'If you haven't posted it yet just give it to me. I'll be getting off near the post-office, I'll put it in the mail myself.'

'Oh really? You seriously expect me to hand over my wife's letter to you, do you? What kind of person are you, asking for another man's wife's letter?'

'Oh, don't worry. I'm not going to open your letter and read it. I was just asking in case you forget . . .'

'What business is it of yours if I do forget?' Harshabardhan wanted to slap the man resoundingly.

'Well, the letter's missing, and then it's the missus's letter, a double mistake, you might say . . .'

'Should I rip it up in front of your eyes? Will that satisfy you?'

'No, spare me, please.' The man got off the tram near the General Post Office.

Harshabardhan ran into Gobardhan as he was climbing the stairs to his home.

'Boudi's at the movies. Have you posted her letter, Dada?'

'So your heart's bleeding for your sister-in-law? Why don't you post the letter yourself? Here it is.'

'There's a postbox right in front of the house. And you can't even remember to post a letter.' Gobra left with the letter.

Harshabardhan heaved a sigh of relief as he took his coat off in his room and hung it up on a hook.

At once the mystery was unravelled.

A piece of paper was pinned to the back of the coat. On it was written in his wife's divine hand: 'Please remind me my husband to post the letter.'

19

How Gobardhan Catches a Thief

'Advertisements do work.'

Harshabardhan sat down heavily in my deckchair, and said this with a sigh of relief.

'Yes, they're definitely not adverse to your prospects – using them is most advisable,' I said without sounding adversarial.

'You remember I made you write the text for an advertisement in the papers the other day?'

'Of course I do,' I answered. 'The one for a night watchman, right?'

'We have a lot of money in our cashbox every day from the day's sales. We can't bring the money home – it's deposited in the bank the next day. Which is why we wanted a capable person to guard the money at night . . .'

'A competent guard for the entire night. I remember clearly,' I said. 'I wrote the copy, after all. Did the advertisement prove useful?'

'You bet it did. That's what I came running to tell you.'

'In fact, it wasn't just useful, it was newsful too,' added Gobra. 'A newspaper ad, after all.'

'How many applications?' I asked.

'Just one for now,' answered Harshabardhan. 'I'm expecting more. But just the one for now.'

'One person applied, and the entire neighbourhood replied. What a sensation!' Gobra wasn't making much sense.

'Two hundred rupees for a two-inch advertisement. But let them take the money. Who pays for two inches anyway?'

'A two hundred rupee advertisement usually means making two hundred times as much money.'

'He made plenty of money. Much more than two hundred times.'

'Nearly six hundred times – isn't that right, Dada?' The younger brother calculated in his head. 'Didn't the box have some sixty-thousand rupees?'

'Closer to eighty thousand. Cleared out.'

'How many times does eighty thousand make?' Gobra calculated percentages in the sky with his finger.

My meagre brains grew numb over their numbers. 'Cleared out?' I asked Harshabardhan. 'What do you mean?'

'Our advertisement came out in yesterday's newspaper, right? And last night thieves broke into our shop and took away all the money. When I unlocked the front door this morning I found the cashbox broken.'

'What!' I was shocked. 'Have you informed the police?'

'What use will that be? They will arrest me instead. They will harass us so badly that we'll have our backs to the wall. Should I look after the business or take care of the police? And I know very well how successfully they will catch the thief.'

'I could catch the thief,' said Gobra, 'but my brother won't let me.'

'You think it's so simple? They have daggers, don't they? They'll stab you if you try to catch them. Rip your belly apart. How do you expect me to allow a naive young man to be knifed?'

'How can I expect such a thing?' I admitted. 'At our age a wife is sharper than a knife.'

'But I would have caught him without any effort. Not with daggers but with detection.'

'How would you have caught him?'

'By following ground rules.'

'Oh, did the fellow leave his footprints on the ground?' I asked curiously. 'Did he dig his own grave by leaving his footprints behind?'

'My foot!' Harshabardhan grimaced. 'Not even a sole sign of the thief. How will your precious detection work?'

'Not the ground outside the shop door,' explained Gobardhan, smiling, 'but ground realities. That's how I will catch the thief. The advertisement ran us aground, didn't it? I have plenty of ground for my confidence.'

I could not fathom the mystery. Nor could Gobra's fat brother. 'Oh yes, Gobra will catch a thief. Indeed.' He paused and then continued, 'Then why hasn't he caught one before? This isn't the first time something of ours has been stolen.'

'You've had things stolen before too?'

'Yes. I myself was stolen,' Harshabardhan told me.

'Are you your own thing?' Gobra protested. 'You belong to Boudi. You're not your own man.'

'Same thing,' his brother snorted. 'You were stolen too, along with me. And you belong to me. I'm your guardian, am I not? Why couldn't you catch the thief then?'

'But what happened? How did you escape from the thief?' I asked.

'The same way that everyone else does. Haven't you heard of stolen goods being robbed? We went from the hands of thieves into the arms of robbers.'

'Indeed?' I asked in amusement. 'But you managed to escape eventually, didn't you? You had no choice. That's the custom of detective stories. But who rescued you?'

'A dacoit appeared. Whereupon the robber ran away in panic.'

'Dacoits on top of robbers?'

'Yes. As soon as Gobra's sister-in-law came home and started shrieking at the front door, the robber took one look and vanished. Through the back door. My wife is as fierce as a dacoit.'

'Fierce? No one fears Boudi,' said Gobra, 'besides you.'

'I'm afraid you're wrong, even robbers are afraid of her,' retorted his brother.

'Never mind,' I tried to mediate in the family argument. 'Don't forget to tell me the story of how you were stolen. I made a little money writing about your war exploits, now this one too might . . .'

'All in good time. Now I'm off to buy a steel safe for the shop. Even if the thief were to come back, he wouldn't find it easy to crack the safe.'

Gobardhan arrived the next morning. 'We're putting this advertisement in the papers today, can you check it for me?'

Gobardhan handed over his epoch-making work of literature.

Mentioning the address of their house in Chetla, the advertisement said, 'Private detective needed. Priceless collection of gems in room with drainpipe running up to the window. Detective must ensure no one climbs up drainpipe. Suitable compensation.'

'I see,' I nodded. 'Just as water resists water, you want to do something similar. As soon as your thief returns to climb up the drainpipe, your detective will catch him in the act. Am I right?'

'You won't get it. It's too complicated for you,' Gobra fired a parting shot before departing.

A few days later a strange man appeared and said, 'Come with me. quick.'

I was flabbergasted by this invitation from a stranger. 'Do I . . . er . . . do I know you?'

'You can't recognize me because I'm in disguise,' said the man, removing his moustache and beard.

'Oh, it's Gobra. But why in this strange garb?'

'I'm off to catch a thief, you see. Detectives have to move about in disguise, don't they? I've got a set of false moustache and beard for you too, put them on quickly.'

'Me? Why me?'

'You have to be in disguise too. You're my assistant. Like Smith's Blake or Holmes's Watson. Since you're my satellite you have to . . .'

'Yours is enough, I don't need any. Everyone knows I don't consort with bearded men. If I'm in your company no one will suspect me of being me.'

'Then come along quickly. We'll do a quick survey of the market. Dada's over there too. That's another reason for the disguise, so that he doesn't recognize me.'

'Right.' We left. As we were passing the shops in the market, Gobra suddenly pinioned a customer at one of them and started shouting, 'Got him. I've caught the thief. Go fetch a policeman quickly.'

The man had done no harm at all. He was merely haggling over the price of chocolate with the shopkeeper when Gobra pounced on him. I felt most uncomfortable.

The man began to scream in terror. And Gobra began to shout too at the top of his voice, calling for his brother and sister-in-law. His false moustache and beard fell off.

Harshabardhan was somewhere nearby. Identifying his brother's voice, he appeared on the spot. 'What is it? Why are you bellowing like a bull?'

'Because I've caught your thief – here he is. You manage him now.'

The man flung himself at Harshabardhan's feet. 'I beg of you babu, don't turn me in to the police. For god's sake. I just got out after doing two years – they'll put me inside for six this time.'

'Very well, we won't. Return everything you stole,' Gobra said threateningly.

'I'll return everything, everything.' The man took us to his shanty gratefully, returning a bundle of notes. Harshabardhan's eighty thousand rupees.

'And my gems? Where are they?' Gobra asked aggressively.

'There, in that corner, babu. Please take them back.'

I saw a couple of boxes in the corner of the room. Peeping into them, I discovered . . . 'Are these your . . .?'

'Gems,' completed Gobardhan. 'Cadbury's Gems. Priceless because no one can resell them, though the thief was trying to.'

20

Gobardhan Follows Instructions

The cat was proving to be a nuisance. No matter where Harshabardhan went, it was always there. He could sense its presence at every step, its tail raised like a flag. It slipped between his feet whenever it could, and brushed his legs with its tail at every opportunity. It would be hard to find another cat so intent on stepping on someone's toes.

The cat irritated Harshabardhan all the time. It disappeared with the fish-head from his plate and finished his bowl of milk. And the less said about the things it did at night after forcing itself under his quilt the better. The sheets had to be changed every day, the quilt had to be washed regularly. How long could he go on this way?

But his wife loved the cat. She spoilt it silly. A little discipline in childhood would have made it change its way, but it was too late now. No one dared touch it.

The other day he discovered that the sofa on which he read his newspaper in comfort every morning was occupied by the cat. Just as he was about to pick it up by the ear and toss it away, his wife rushed in.

'What do you think you're doing? A cat's ears should never be touched. Cats die if you do that, they cannot stand having their ears boxed. They aren't schoolboys, you know.'

'Of course not, they're suitors for your daughter's hand,' he replied angrily. 'We have to treat your cat like a resident son-in-law. Just let it come near my feet again, I'll give it such a kick – that will teach it a lesson.'

'Don't you dare! Lay a hand on the cat and I'll go to my mother's.' Instead of the cat, it was Harshabardhan whom she threatened with dire consequences.

Harshabardhan couldn't find his chequebook. He had to withdraw a large sum of money for some urgent work, but the entire chequebook had vanished. He scoured the desk, the drawers, the cupboards – even Gobardhan's pockets – but it was nowhere to be found. Eventually it was discovered – on a table – beneath the cat.

The cat was curled up cosily on it.

When he got his hands on the cheque-book he used it to whack the cat, whereupon it shrieked loudly and jumped off the table.

Harshabardhan's wife came running from the kitchen at the sound of her cat's agonized yowling. 'Who hit the cat? Cats shouldn't be hit.' She cradled it in her arms. 'Cats are the favourite of the Goddess Shashthi.'

'Tit for tat.'

'Tit for tat? Whatever for?'

'My cheque-book is no less a favourite of the Goddess Lakshmi's. Is the goddess of wealth less important than the goddess of children? My favourite has given your favourite a thrashing. Tit for tat.'

Without prolonging the argument, Harshabardhan's wife said, 'Have some milk,' to the cat and took it away.

'Gobra!' Harshabardhan shouted for his brother.

'What is it, Dada?' Gobra came out of his room.

'How can you allow me to suffer this way? So much humiliation!'

'What's the matter, Dada?'

'Can you not fill the gap left by a mere cat? Is that how useless you are? Even more of a failure than a feline?'

'What are you talking about?' Gobra could make no sense of all this.

'Your sister-in-law loves animals because she has no children of her own – don't you have any feelings?'

Gobra's mouth fell open. He didn't know what to say. Perhaps we wanted to display his fillings – in his teeth.

'Can't you meet your sister-in-law's need to mother someone, Gobra?'

'How can I? I'm not a little baby who can climb into her lap. I can't do that, Dada.'

'Is there no other way to love a child? You're so close to her – you could very well follow her around just like the cat.'

'No, Dada. I can't be a cat.'

'I'm not asking you to be one. And you couldn't even if you tried. You might be able to crawl, or even mew – but can you grow a tail?'

'I'd better not grow one.' Gobra did not appear excited by his brother's proposal.

'So I'm not asking you to be a cat. I'm asking you to be adopted like a cat. If you were to be adopted . . .'

'What are you saying, Dada! I'm your brother. You want to adopt your brother?' Gobra protested.

'What harm can it do? The scriptures say an elder brother is like a father. That means your sister-in-law is like your mother. Isn't that so?'

'Boudi, just listen to what Dada is saying,' Gobardhan shouted.

Harshabardhan's wife came running from the kitchen. She couldn't believe what she heard.

'Have you gone mad? How can your brother be your adopted son? You might turn me into your mother-in-law one day. You're going senile.'

'It's entirely possible. Your cat has made me mad.' Harshabardhan sulked.

'The cat didn't bite you, did it?' asked Gobra anxiously. 'I believe you can go mad from a cat bite. The way you thrash it every now and then, it could easily bite you even if it hasn't yet.'

'Let it. Serves him right. He won't try to fight with my cat after that,' said Harshabardhan's wife.

'No Boudi, it won't serve him right. Dog bites lead to hydrophobia, you can't drink water any more, and you just bark all the time. A cat bite might lead to milkophobia. He might mew constantly. And when someone suffering from hydrophobia bites someone else, that person also gets hydrophobia and begins to bark . . .'

'Let the cat bite, I'd be happy if it did,' declared Harshabardhan. 'The first person I'd bite is your sister-in-law.'

'That would be terrible!' Gobra couldn't contain himself. 'If both of you start behaving like cats, who will bell the cat?'

'You, of course,' said Harshabardhan grimly. 'You, brother Gobardhan.'

'Never heard of such a thing in my life.' Harshabardhan's wife went back to the kitchen.

Harshabardhan brooded, while Gobardhan looked guilty. He felt responsible for the affair of the cat.

'There's something you can do,' said Harshabardhan after some thought. 'That will ensure you don't have to bell the cat. It will get rid of the beast and give us some respite too.'

'But I won't have to fill the space left behind by the cat, will I?'

'No, not at all,' Harshabardhan assured his brother. 'Not now. I'll tell you tomorrow morning, when your sister-in-law goes to the river for her holy dip.'

The next morning, when Harshabardhan's wife was away, he told Gobardhan, 'She isn't home now. Get rid of the cat.'

'What! When she finds out she won't spare me.'

'Provided she finds out. How will she know we got rid of it? The cat's not going to come back and tell her.'

'Boudi won't eat unless the cat's by her side.'

'What can we do about that? Cats are whimsical, they wander away, they never settle down in one place. They're always trying the food in different houses – who knows where the cat might have gone. They keep walking away, that's why it's called a catwalk.'

'That's true. Cats are always scatting off,' agreed Gobra.

'There you are then. Take the cat somewhere far away and abandon it. Nowhere nearby. It'll find its way back in that case.'

'Where should I take it?'

'To Howrah.'

'Put it on a train, you mean?'

'Of course not. Just cross the river and to Howrah. Abandon it deep inside some neighbourhood there. But be careful! Don't go there directly. Change buses thrice. Take the bus from Chetla, then the tram from Kidderpore to Shyambazar via Esplanade. To Shyambazar or to Baghbazar. Then to Chitpore, and then across the Howrah Bridge. On the other side you can go in one of three directions – towards Shibpur or Salkia or Bandhaghat. Whichever you prefer.'

'All right. And then?'

'Then take the road that lies straight ahead – take the cat along. There will be a lane on the right . . .'

'What if there isn't one?'

'Then take the one on the left. Where there's a road there's a lane, and where there's a lane there are more lanes. Take every lane, every bylane, don't say 'bye to the lanes . . . and then leave the cat outside a house that looks like one where it will be looked after and fed well. Run away as soon as you let it go, don't forget.'

'Why should I run away? Who am I afraid of?'

'The cat might follow you, you see. Take a long and winding route back through the same lanes. Make sure that cat doesn't follow you.'

'I'll take the rickshaesque-busque route. Rickshaws and buses. I don't need you tell me.'

'Then off you go. Here's a hundred rupees for expenses.' Harshabardhan counted out ten ten-rupee notes for his brother.

Pocketing the money and socketing the cat under his arm, Gobardhan left.

Harshabardhan's wife looked for her cat when she returned. She wanted to sprinkle a little holy water on the cat, but it was nowhere to be found. It waited for this ritual every day, but where had it gone today?

'Where's pussy?' she asked her husband.

'How should I know, I don't keep track of pussy,' Harshabardhan said with a straight face. 'Do you suppose it tells me where it goes?'

'But it doesn't doesn't go anywhere. It's always home. A darling.'

'An ape.'

'Don't abuse my pussy cat, all right? I'm warning you. Where has it gone to – I've brought holy water.'

'No need to purify your cat. Your good deeds are enough – it will go to heaven hanging on to your tailcoat.'

'What a horrible thing to say. Where's it gone to?'

She combed the house, looking beneath the bed, in the corners behind the cupboards and the drawers, everywhere – but not even its tail was to be seen.

She made enquiries with the neighbours – the wretched thing wasn't at any of their houses either. The neighbours said they were troubled enough by their own cats, and had no inclination to provide shelter to another cat.

Harshabardhan's wife had no appetite at lunch, dawdling over her slice of fish, wondering where her cat was.

When her husband tried to remind her that the true home of fish was the human stomach and not the plate, she snarled at him. 'You made my cat leave home. I hope it hasn't committed suicide.'

'I hope it has,' her husband replied. 'I'll perform the last rites with great fanfare.'

Evening was approaching. Harshabardhan began to worry. Not for the cat, but for his brother.

Where was Gobra? He hadn't been run over by a bus or a tram in trying to get rid of the cat, had he?

Evening turned into night. No sign of Gobra.

His lunch was still on the table. Where was Thakurpo? Now Harshabardhan's wife also began to fret about her brother-in-law – he was never so late.

Her anxiety for her cat was now replaced by anxiety for her brother-in-law. Where could he have disappeared? Finally she took a taxi to go looking for him – and to enquire with relatives and at the police station and the hospitals.

Harshabardhan was at home, stupefied. Had he lost his brother in his attempts to get rid of the cat? Tears streamed from his eyes.

Suddenly Gobardhan appeared, with unkempt hair and a drawn face, looking bedraggled.

'How long you've been away! It's ten at night. Where have you been?'

'I did what you asked me to . . . all those lanes and by lanes . . .'

'But that was to get there. You could have taken a shortcut on the way back. Jumped into the first bus or taxi.'

'That's all very well, but I lost my way.'

'How did you get home, then?'

'I followed the cat.'